WHERE THE DINOSAURS ROAM

EDDIE GENEROUS

SEVEREDPRESS

WHERE THE DINOSAURS ROAM

Copyright © 2022 by Eddie Generous

WWW.SEVEREDPRESS.COM

ISBN: 978-1-922861-43-6

1974 – 73 YEARS AGO

Dr. Pierre Racicot couldn't look at his wife a moment longer. He saw his son's face in her face. The high cheekbones and dimpled chin, the subtle cat-like tilt to her eyes, their son had inherited it all. Every day was a fresh cut with a dull blade.

Pierre also saw his wife's country, a country he'd called home for the last twenty-one years, a country that had snatched their only child and sent him into a foreign jungle. That jungle ate him up and spit out a notification to be passed along by an officer and a chaplain. And for what? To further stretch capitalism's reach? To keep a country on the other side of the planet from adopting a different financial system?

Those men had said sorry in a way that was canned, rehearsed hundreds of times over. Pierre had spit on the chaplain's Bible after knocking it from his hand. The escalation was immediate. The officer withdrew his service pistol and pressed it to the doctor's forehead. "I'm sorry for your loss, but he died in service of the greatest country in the world. A Christian nation. Blasphemy, and disrespect of the Lord, will not be tolerated."

"Send me to your devil then," Pierre said, flinching but a modicum. "Satan has more heart than any rail-thin waif nailed to a cross."

The officer sneered, his body tense, but ultimately holstered the weapon the moment Henrietta Racicot came into view beyond her husband. Her shoes clicked against the stone of the foyer, one, two, three steps before she understood the most significant point of the scene before her and fainted dead away. Pierre looked from the men with their brazen threats and empty condolences to the human heap on the floor behind him.

Within days, the household had changed drastically. Henrietta had turned to her family and the upbringing she'd begun to ignore since taking up with an atheist. She begged Pierre to join her in the church, join her in prayer, kneel before a pale lord. "Please. Please," she said, face tear smeary, looking up from the floor of their bedroom, hands clasped together. "He is our salvation. He will give us strength."

Pierre sneered at the display and retreated to his garage where he'd been working on something scientists had been piecing together since the dawn of individual enlightenment. The following Sunday, Henrietta left with her parents for service, and Pierre made quick work of packing their AMC Ambassador station wagon. He left behind an envelope with $5,000 in cash and a note that read: *Rely not on the pie in the sky. Man is alone. Man can depend on only himself.*

The trek was long, and yet felt as if only moments passed, his mind so full. Sixteen hours after departing, Pierre arrived at his family's deserted home—a parcel of land he'd kept for a time of need; though he'd assumed that need would be more like an investment than what it would become. He used the faded brass key he'd carried on his keyring since leaving for Berkley in 1952. The lock was rusty, but functional. He dropped the thick chains and pushed open the squeaky iron gates. The grass along the lane was tall and windblown, like the hair of a baby whisking over a mostly bald cranium. The asphalt of the skinny driveway was cracked, weeds sprouting like wayward cowlicks. He pulled ahead thirty yards to the front door of the home where he'd grown up and engaged the car's parking brake.

He whistled in surprise looking up at the broken windows. A tall spruce tree had fallen through the roof into the living room, leaving in its wake a gaping hole that was now fuzzy with a pelt of thick, green moss. He'd expected downfall, but this complete ruination bit deep into him. Of course, it had been long on its way to destruction when he'd left—his parents had moved out of the home proper in 1949, one day after the USSR announced the successful detonation of First Lightning—an atomic bomb.

Only briefly did he wonder what his childhood bedroom looked like now. An image flashed of him sitting on his bed, reading something by Isaac Asimov, his mother coming in to call him to lunch. The scene made him wince. There was no time for that, not with the steel case in the back of the station wagon steadily warming closer to instability.

His parents' obsessive fear of nuclear technologies obviously had some effect on him. As terrified of atomic possibilities as his parents had been, he'd become equally as intrigued by their power and usefulness.

Out of the car, he took the plutonium case from the trunk and started around the side yard to the hill at the rear of the house and toward the bald spot on the lawn. The green paint had faded, but the long grass also lacked vibrancy, as if the bunker hatch were a chameleon or that the grass itself was trying to match a tone. He set the case down carefully as he knelt to consider the combination lock. He'd known it, but only now did he wonder if they'd changed the code at some point. If they had, his plan was done before it began because time was oh, oh so short now—the case felt like fresh sunshine on already burned flesh. He set the case down so, so gently.

12. 17. 99.

The locking mechanism clicked open, and Pierre spun the hatch wheel. The door was heavy, screeching, several inches of steel on a hinge in need of oiling. The air rising toward him was stale, but the coolness was evident and welcome, necessary if he wasn't going to melt himself into a puddle. A pent breath escaped Pierre's chest in a grateful sigh. If this had failed, and the stolen plutonium in the steel case destabilized, there would have been an incredible mess. Though, of course, he'd be inadvertently answering a question the other professors at Berkley would be almost too terrified to consider if this failed.

"Should've left a note. *Promise I won't blow anybody up but myself,*" he said and nearly laughed in that hopeless way belonging solely to the overwrought and emotionally exhausted.

He again took the case by the handle and began down the ramp into the bunker where both his parents had succumbed to cancer. He flicked a light switch, hope, hope, hoping he still had power. The light flickered to life.

Just behind the property, the Overseer Mountain icefield had countless creeks and streams, both above and below ground. Some of which harbored hidden generators that, apparently, were still powering the bunker. Pierre took five steps deeper into the small space and huffed an exhalation, causing his cheeks to flare. Tobacco stains oozed down the pale green walls like hideous paint blobs. Terrified of the energy of the future, but fully willing to poison themselves with countless carcinogens of today. That was his shortsighted parents.

Shelves lined the walls of the twenty-by-twenty space, most of them empty. There were cans of food and jugs of water, though there was also running water, the source deep, deep down into the stone beneath the bunker and safe—according to his father. His father had rented a bulldozer when the paranoia first began to settle within him. The bunker was in a natural crater, the dirt went in around the great steel belly he'd planted like a tulip bulb. Pierre's mother seeded the new soil, watered it, raised the grass thereon like it was a second child.

At first, it had been a little fun, the engineering aspect of this strange backyard project with his father, figuring out the power and water. The man wasn't overly wise, but he was wise enough to listen to his teenage son and the books on loan from the library up in Pemberton. Eventually, the paranoia became an embarrassment to Pierre—everyone worried a little over what America had done to the Japanese and what the repercussions might come to be, but they still lived because nuclear warfare was out of their control. His parents, however, retreated from society aside from grocery deliveries to the house; paid for by cash left in the mailbox. Young men in grocer outfits would arrive at the front door of the failing home and leave behind bags of necessities.

"This'll do," Pierre said now, eyes closed to the bunker around him, seeing what he'd come to build in the impending months. He set down the case and started away. There was a ton of work to do yet before he got to the dangerous step.

—

The old home was good for recyclable materials to build above the hatch. He couldn't live down there, not next to the plutonium. As it was, he could only spend forty minutes at a time putting together the pieces of his vision—his vision by way of dozens of educated but failed visions prior. One did not stand alone in the field of science.

Out of the mess, they'd come together as one and he'd get back to a time before his son was taken and correct that single string of events that caused the senseless death and unbearable grief. There'd be no stopping Hitler or the colonizer slave trade, no plans of slowing capitalistic rule or mental clouding by religious force. He'd save his son and history would be only a hair off its natural course.

By day ninety, after arriving, he had a small cottage on a hill with a hidden door that led to the bunker, he had the schematic of his end goal worked out, and he had lost his hair and several teeth, which would hardly matter when he went back in time to speak with himself.

For the last few weeks, he'd been pushing it down there, working nine or ten forty-minute shifts in a day, tinkering, experimenting. Even now he drank salted water and forced down two spoons full of beans while he wore only a tinfoil suit, ready to return to the radioactive project for another try. Though this time, he would not go alone.

He opened the trapdoor to the bunker hatch and climbed down, the small painted turtle with eight feet of rope wrapped around its belly tucked beneath his arm like a pigskin. He immediately slipped once though the hatch. In his weakened state, everything was becoming trouble, especially when the task involved equilibrium. He swallowed at the fuzziness rising up into the back of his throat. The turtle slipped from his grip, falling over the edge of the ramp, when he reached back to pull the hatch closed behind him. Luckily, the strap was wrapped enough around Pierre's wrist that the animal never hit the floor below.

"Whoa, now," he said, taking several deep breaths while trying to gain a semblance of control.

Thin blood trailed over his bottom lip as he regained his footing and shuffled down to the floor. To his left and to his right were the shelves. The food and water had been removed. Now on the shelves were great coils of wire, radios riding nearly imperceptible frequencies, and tractor batteries connected to the creek chargers piling into the bunker from all around the property and adjacent mountain. Landed on firm ground, Pierre's knees tried to buckle. He was running out of time; this would have to be a short visit...unless of course the turtle survived going through the portal wall at the back of the bunker.

The portal looked like a fog bank, tacked strangely in place, though moving and unstable. Sluggish and short of breath, Pierre crossed the space, dragging the turtle behind him by the rope. He spat a mouthful of metallic-tasting saliva onto the steel floor. A tooth pinged and bounced out through the portal.

"You're up," he said to the turtle.

Pierre bent and snatched the small thing as it attempted a futile escape. His head swooned and he toppled sideways, dropping to a knee, his shoulder heavy against a wall of batteries. He reared back and tossed the turtle through the portal, the rope firm around his right wrist. His puffy tongue rimmed his dry and flaking lips as he lifted his left arm to watch the second hand of his Bulova turn slowly around its scratched and cloudy face. After a minute, he began reeling in the turtle. The animal was completely within its shell when it popped over the ledge. Pierre watched and waited. If it was dead, there would be no going over, not yet, he'd need to tweak it. Trepid, with calculated slowness, the turtle head pushed from its shell. It had gone somewhere into the past, now Pierre needed only a baseline to adjust time on the far side of the portal. He pushed to his feet, unthinking that the rope remained connected to his wrist. One step, two, he entered the fog bank of the portal and light shined down upon him immediately.

He squinted, looking about. Instantly, he understood that he'd gone too far. Around him were the natural walls of the crater. They were sandy, naked.

He'd gone back to a time before his parents and their bunker, but by how far back?

Pierre put his hands down and monkey crawled up the side of the crater, carving the loose walls, creating a trail. The crater was indeed newish, and no longer seemed the obvious result of glacial movements. He reached the top and pushed to sit upon the ledge. So short of breath, panic struck, and he scrambled to get the suit's hood off. He inhaled deeply, stretching back to let his energy catch up to his movements. That air was good and clean. On his side, it was then that he noticed the turtle's rope. He dragged the animal up to the ledge.

"Go on," he whispered after releasing the animal, though not untying the rope from its shell.

His throat scratched and the words felt like a cheese grater against the meat of his lungs. Not far away, he heard running water. Above all else right now, he needed a drink. On hands and knees, he followed his ears. All around him, things were different. The plants had been super-sized. Great orange mushrooms sprouted like trees. Footprints of mysterious beasts created deep, deep stamps into the firm earth beneath him. Distantly, animal cries rang high, at octaves unusual to the animals of his time. Still, all he could think about was the water; some troubles were absolute.

The flow grew louder, as did splashing footfalls. Animals honked. Animals snorted. Pierre had eyes only for his hands beneath him. Whatever those animals were, whenever they were from, none of that mattered until he satiated his parched throat and mouth.

Cool, his hands found mud. A small thrill played up his chest. Mud meant he was close. Four more steps and his arms sank more than a foot and his face dipped into cool, murky water. It was glorious, but unexpected. He sucked and swallowed. He coughed against the need that had him overindulging. Still, he went back for more. This water was magic, and Pierre had the clear but useless thought: this water had a great deposit of some silky element, perhaps silicone or possibly a simple lack of calcium. It soothed like no drink before it ever had.

Satiated, Pierre rolled to his side, sinking into the mud. So cool, so comforting. He closed his eyes.

—

Pierre awoke with gooey eyes and a throbbing headache. Evening had settled over the world, leaving everything golden-hued and dreamlike. He lifted a hand to his face, his flesh felt puffy and vaguely dissociated from his nervous system, as if the radiation poisoning were breaking some connections, while building up those that carried pained messages. He looked about himself, finally drinking in the reality of where he was, or rather, when he was. A huge grey forest rose like redwoods but weren't right, and he'd mostly left those kinds of trees in his wake when he'd returned to Canada. Those were California and Oregon trees—they were here and there in BC, though were only spotted in with a variety of spruce up this far north. Here was a thick wall of almost identical stalks that rose and rose and rose— not quite redwoods, but close enough to assume a familial link. The mushrooms, he'd never seen anything like them. They were big, incredibly so, almost like a dream plucked from Lewis Carroll's mind. The crater he'd climbed from wasn't a crater at all but was a sand dune, perhaps even the result of a meteorite rather than glacial movement.

"Overshot," he said, his voice raspy.

Thoughts of the silky water came to him, and he let the world be for a moment, leaning in and pressing his cheek to the cool surf, slurping down the soothing drink. He used his left hand as a cup and brought the water in to his face so that he didn't pitch forward, go under. He lifted his abdomen and caught the reflection of a large bird circling far overhead. It was big as an eagle, though had a swinging tail and longer legs. A snort played out across the water—a pond of about fifty yards from center to every shore. Scaly with a long skinny face, plump in the middle. It had beady eyes and an ugly beak. Further back behind it were a half-dozen bird-like creatures chasing it down, or perhaps simply chasing it away. It seemed unlikely the small animals would trail this larger one in the game of hunter and prey.

"Bird hyenas," he whispered when he saw the great spreading bloodstain upon the water as the big lizard entered. The bird-like creatures hissed and danced at the opposite shore of the pond. "Dinosaurs."

That big creature, though injured, was coming closer. It looked like an herbivore, but that did not mean pleasant or peaceful. Pierre had once listened to the story of a wealthy classmate's father who had gone on an African hunting expedition. The man had shot a lion and was on his way out of the jungle when his team encroached on the territory of a pack of water buffalo. The buffalo attacked and destroyed all but the guides who could act quickly enough where the hunters, though warned of this possibility, simply were not ready.

He rolled to his hands and knees, both palms sinking into pale brown mud. His vision swam as the blood seemed to rush away from his brain. Still, he pushed on like a drunkard tossed from a pub. Great honks and squeaks echoed around him and he blindly groped on, pushing, pushing, pushing away from this world. He had to be at least 100,000,000 years earlier than he'd hoped, possibly more. He'd been so focused on making it back, he hadn't considered that he'd go so far into the past, that first hurdle of simple success was too big to see around from the moderate safety of 1974.

His lungs burned and saliva drooled in great ropes from his puffy, crusty lips, the fluids playing up his throat and down from his sinus. Blinded by desire, he now had to acknowledge that he'd spent far too much time in the bunker in a short span. And what was his rush? A time machine gave him mastery over the universe's hourglass, or it would have. Grief had made him stupid.

His swimming vision found steady footing, but his arms failed to keep him balanced, and he flopped into stiff sand. Footfalls shot dust and pebbles into his cheeks. Pierre turned his face and exhaled an exhausted breath. Those three-foot bird-like beasts had come around the pond. The injured herbivore would not be his undoing.

A word came to mind, and though he'd never heard of a dinosaur with feathers, he hissed, "Raptor," a moment before one snatched at his right hand. It pulled him a foot from where he lay, his flesh torn beneath the sharp, sharp beak. He wailed in pain. The raptors wailed back, giving a screeching goose's war-crying over his anguish. Another snapped at his left foot, pulling, tugging, yanking him in the opposite direction until removing most of his slacks in a single rip.

"Forgive me!" Pierre shouted to the son he'd never save from the American war machine. He inhaled deeply and opened his mouth to say more but words failed him. Mid-scream, he lay in the sand, ruffled and sweaty shirt on his back, bloodied boxer shorts covering his hips, holey socks, one shoe…this was the end and there was nothing he could do about it but scream. He began to laugh hysterically in-between bouts of pain. This was like being beaten to death by second graders with sharp sticks. "End this!" He pushed to sit up but immediately tottered, pitching to his left.

His breaths came in and out on short panting flashes. He waited and waited and waited, but the raptors were leaving him alone. He peeked through his left eye, spotting one of the beasts more than twenty feet away now. It wasn't quite looking at him. Pierre let his gaze play downward, into the gulley throat of a massive crocodile that had come upon him in silence. Its huge teeth snapped onto his thighs and yanked him toward the pond. He screamed a non-word, holding the sound until his throat blew out and he spewed out great jellied chunks of clotted blood—the radiation had played irreversible games with his cells and organs. The crocodile continued sprinting in reverse until Pierre was submerged in the silky water. He felt bottom with his forehead as he spun in the grip of a death roll. In a blink, he saw his son, he saw his wife, he saw his first lover, he saw his first cat, his first microscope, his first day of school. It had come and gone so, so quickly, and from the viewpoint at the bottom of a prehistoric pond, he'd wasted his life.

"Forgive me," he said, or thought he did and then inhaled deeply. The silky water filled his lungs. The crocodile continued spinning for twelve more revolutions—this prey would die easier than the usual offerings. Within a minute, the crocodile was back topside, and once to the shallows, it let Pierre's corpse go. It repositioned its hold, taking him down in nine bites. All that remained when the beast was through was a stubby bit of torn rope and a single shoe.

From where it burrowed into the sand, the painted turtle watched, unaware that it was not where it belonged.

ONE

On the holo tablet in the security guard's hands, a newscaster was wishing Aubrey Plaza a happy fifty-second birthday. A video montage ran through images from her films, red carpet appearances, and a few from her personal life—undoubtedly, all would look and sound pretty much the same. The guard swiped it away after about ten seconds, and then continued swiping without giving another piece of hologram imagery time to rise from the tablet.

Hannah Laurie watched this from where she stood in the lobby of the apartment building where she'd lived the last five years with her daughter, Skylar, and her son, Gabe. It had been a nice enough place, and a steal given where housing costs had gone more recently. She couldn't help but wonder what would become of the family, wonder and hope. The news wasn't all bad.

She awaited the Dìzhǔ Corporation's men to arrive and hand off her check. At the time she'd signed the lease, the provincial government had been enforcing landlords to offer current renters and new renters price-fix options for up to fifteen-year periods in an effort to keep Vancouver liveable—liveable in a more traditional sense than where it appeared to be headed. With a change in government came a change in rules. All apartment units, single dwelling and multiple dwelling residential units, and business fronts of fewer than ten floors, could be vacated and up zoned, offering the displaced individuals a refund of 50% of what they'd paid in rent since signing the lease while potentially incurring other penalties on top. The Dìzhǔ Corporation would have no trouble recouping the losses with new leases.

"Hey, good looking."

Hannah turned and gave her neighbor a half-smile. The woman speaking was named Annette. She was carrying a box loaded with household bric-a-brac, a brass lamp towering above the rest of the stuff like a temple built on an island of junk.

"How you doing?" Hannah said.

"Fine, I guess. Don't think I've ever seen you in blue jeans."

Hannah looked down at the decade-old pair of Guess Jeans she wore. She didn't recall the last time she'd put them on. Moving was dirty, irritating business, though now it came with a pleasant side, a stirring of butterflies. Not having to doll up to leave her space was completely understandable if she was in the middle of a move. Normally, even standing on the sidelines at Gabe's school demanded that she dress her part—many parents watching from the sidelines had money, and business opportunities arose any and all hours of the day. Working on commission meant she had to look the part of endless professionalism and availability.

"I tried a skirt, but I showed off too much when I bent over," Hannah said, putting on one of her most winning expressions, the one that said *we're on the same team.*

"Right. So, you find a place?" Annette said.

The expression slipped from Hannah's face. "No. Me and the kids are leaving the city, going to look at some places this afternoon."

"Wish I could leave." Annette looked into the box of stuff like it might have the answers to her troubles. She was older, somewhere between fifty-five and seventy, depending on her skin care regimen.

Hanna frowned. "How long you been here?"

"Thirty-two years."

To the outsider looking in, the payout deal sounded all right. What nobody seemed to feel like acknowledging was that people who'd lived in rentals from before the time of the government's handy lease stipulation hadn't signed anything new and were being grandfathered out, by and by. Annette would get exactly squat for her eviction and she'd be looking for a place to live that might demand a 20x cost hike.

"I'm so sorry," Hannah said.

"You didn't do anything to be sorry for. I'm the sorry one. After Rodney's payout, we lumped around for so long…I haven't even had a job in ten years."

Rodney had worked a decade in the paint department at a factory that made parts for Ford and Mazda. He and the nine other employees working in his unit, including two other men, had developed breast cancer. This was enough to suggest a precaution had been ignored. The company settled out of court and the case disappeared from the headlines.

"Where will you go?" Hannah said.

Annette sighed. "I don't know. I'm only fifty-eight. The government assisted living places won't take me. I'm on a wait list for a place down in Langley, but the manager suggested I keep getting on other lists because there were three thousand people ahead of me and only a couple spots opened per year. I'll probably need another good virus to go around, wipe out some folks so I can get in somewhere." She smiled humorlessly as she said this. "I'm joking, of course."

Hannah shook her head. This was a bad news scenario people on social media talked about, but the press was ignoring it for the most part—likely thanks to endowments to news outlets from the very same government allowing the changes to the city's bylaws.

"Me and the Bradleys and the Jongs and the Patels went in on a storage locker together. I don't know…they think someone's going to fix the problem. I just want to hold onto my stuff long enough to sell some of it. Not that it's worth anything." Annette finally looked up. "You need any household items?"

Hannah needed nothing from that box of junk or any other old boxes of junk and said, "How much for the lamp?"

Annette put on a forced grin. "Fifty?" The word came out more like a plea than a request.

The lamp was a Walmart special, made in China sticker on the base. Probably cost $15 twenty years ago. Hannah paid the woman and set the lamp down by her feet.

"Good luck," she said. This conversation *had* to be over.

"Yeah, right." Annette put on a faux snooty attitude. "If you're ever in the neighborhood, why don't you stop by my place, Happy Lights. I'd love to entertain guests."

Hannah's mouth tightened against her teeth. "Maybe you'll get in somewhere."

Happy Lights was one of the countless internet café towers that had sprung up in the last decade. People who used the café swiped an identity card attached to a credit card and found themselves a cubicle with a padded bench and a PC. At 90¢ per hour, it was far and away the most affordable way to live, the only way to live for so, so many. Of course, people there had to accept living in a closet and walls that didn't go up to the ceiling, meaning hearing and smelling countless *neighbors* at all hours of the day.

Annette was out of sight by the time the Dìzhǔ Corporation's men came in through the front entrance, all wearing expensively tailored black suits and shiny black loafers. They had matching short black haircuts and clean-shaven faces. Hannah felt a sting of hatred stab into her at that moment. These men and the company they worked for weren't Canadian, but because of money, they got to enter a foreign country and dictate how folks lived.

They continued by Hannah, grinning and nodding to her as they entered what used to be the superintendent's office. Two minutes later, they called her inside. The check was ready, as were the contracts, which included a non-disparagement clause—she was signing away her right to speak negatively about Dìzhǔ Corporation on social media and beyond. Whatever.

The trio of men nodded at her again, grinning. Hannah picked up the check for $201,300 and slipped it into the tight pocket of her jeans. From her other pocket, she withdrew the keys to the apartment. One man held out his hand, palm up.

Hannah tossed the keys onto the desk and said, "Fetch," before she walked away, knowing that $200K wouldn't go far while hoping it would go just far enough to exit halfway comfortably.

TWO

Skylar Laurie was tagging along with an older friend named Abby, who was due to become the resident advisor for the first through fifth floors of the women's dorm at UBC, Vancouver. The second semester was through, and the summer semester was set to begin the following Monday. To ensure their residence spots, students typically rolled three semesters a year until graduation, otherwise they'd have to deal with the housing problem that could be covered by student loans but then bury them in debt for decades after graduation. As it was, the province covered the rooming of every student, should they choose to live on campus—choose being a loose term. Those with the funds to do so typically did not live on campus and lived in one of many of the new high-rise buildings shooting into the skyline. Those who had to, *chose* to live in one of the many residences.

Being around all those college kids and feeling all that potential for freedom had Skylar giddy with anticipation. Come September, she'd be in one of the cubical-sized rooms with a bed, desk, and wardrobe. If she was lucky, she'd get into a solo unit, though anything new and freeing would be close enough to perfection that she could hardly stand still waiting for it. If she hadn't been coming back to the city in a few months, she likely would've had a fit at her mother for moving them out to the suburbs. Knowing her mother didn't have much of a choice and still not blaming her for the move would've been impossible, would've demanded a maturity Skylar had never possessed.

"What you really hope is to get onto a floor that's a multiple of five. The fifth, the tenth, the fifteenth, so on;

the RA from the floor above ignores everything going on below them. Last semester, the thirtieth had the hands down best parties."

Skylar grinned at Abby. She had been to parties, but they rarely happened without supervision, and when they did, the parties were rarely any kind of racy fun, all video games and pizza.

"Guess, though, I'll be one of the bad guys come next week." Abby frowned, though it was a playful frown that shifted into a more serious expression. "You'll have to watch it. I partied too hard and finished with a C average, barely. Seriously, it's why I took the RA spot. It doesn't pay or anything, but I need to focus."

Skylar's grin slipped, though inwardly it remained as big as ever. What happened to Abby had nothing to do with her own future. Some students couldn't handle the freedoms, but she'd been living almost like an adult for years since her mom worked so hard. Her dad had to go—and for once Skylar agreed with her mother, though was too young to have much of an opinion beyond an emotional response at the time—and somebody had needed to watch Gabe while Hannah built up that essential client list. Or as Hannah called it 'her book.'

Skylar's phone vibrated against her thigh, and she slipped it out to check the message. She looked up at Abby. "My mom's on her way."

"You excited about all the space?" Abby said.

People in Vancouver always talked about space with a sense of longing, and for the older crowd, it was longing mixed with nostalgia, but no one wanted to leave the city. It was as if there was an invisible tether that ran from the busy sewer to their hearts, from the busy downtown to their minds, from the busy citizens to their souls. This even when everyone was furious with the provincial government and then, more so, the local government for selling out their chance at a future that looked a bit like their past. Back when $10,000,000 bought a mansion, not a dated bachelor condo with squeaky hinges, ruddy walls, water damaged ceilings, and mice behind the plaster.

"I guess I'll see what it's like. I know I'll be glad to come back to the city when summer's over," Skylar said as they walked toward the stainless-steel elevator doors. They'd been wandering the upper floors and it would take a bit to ride all the way down to the ground. "I'm totally boiled to be coming here."

They rode three floors and the doors opened to a couple young women with skin so white they looked almost porcelain. One said, "Go down?" with a distinctly Eastern European accent—one of those former Soviet kind of vibes.

"Yeah," Abby said.

"Oh, no, no," the one said, and the pair backed out.

"I'm a little envious," Abby said, eyes on the steadily dropping numbers above the sliding doors. "I haven't been out of the city in years. It just costs so much to rent a car and…you know?"

"My mom had to rent a cube truck. It has to get plugged in like every hundred kilometers or something, so we'll be stopping everywhere."

Abby laughed a little. "Your brother and you in a moving truck with your mom driving?"

Skylar tilted her head. "Why's that funny?"

"Your brother's Gabe, right?" Abby said.

The doors opened and two middle-aged women entered. They were both in sweats, hair done in rats' nest chic.

"Yeah?" Skylar said.

Abby shrugged and went back to looking at the falling numbers. "Be a pretty tight fit, especially for a long drive. Your mother find you all a place yet? I know that's never easy."

"No, but the transit train runs all the way from Lillooet. I think she wants to go up that way because most of her clients won't be mad at her if she says she lives outside Whistler. She does investments and insurance, mostly insurance." Skylar was suddenly embarrassed. Her collar was hot, and her cheeks were reddening; it was almost sacrilegious to talk about leaving the city, especially in front of strangers. Almost as bad as talking about working for a living instead of being rich from the onset.

"Oh, yeah. I guess people might get funny about their insurance person leaving the city…though I guess not if it sounds somewhere flashy," Abby said.

One of the middle-aged women half-turned and looked at Skylar. "Soon as I have my degree, I'm going north. Government's hiring all kinds of tree-keepers. You get a whole house to yourself and endless wilderness."

The other woman snorted. "All the tree-keeper business is half the reason there's nowhere good to live."

"Like to breathe, don't you?" the first said.

The second huffed.

"Well, we need forests," the first said.

The doors opened onto the tenth floor and two more young women stepped into the elevator. The capacity was ten, as it was a smallish space, one of a dozen elevators throughout the building. A constant breeze played over the passengers, keeping the air flowing down through the floor, helping to quell some of the droplets leaving mouths that might attack other riders' immune systems. With each pound within the car, the air push increased, making hairs dance and tickling ears.

"I don't think I can stay away from the city," Skylar said.

"I wouldn't want to try," Abby said.

They came to a stop, and all aside from the middle-aged women stepped out. The one who wanted to be a tree-keeper reached for the panel, likely to push the button for one of the subterranean floors—one housed laundry and the other was the main food court.

"Where you headed now?" Skylar said.

Abby shrugged. "Just seeing you out."

Amid the thick traffic, not far from the doors where they stood, was a white cube van sitting high above all else. Skylar squinted and could just barely distinguish her mother behind the wheel through the shimmer of hot glass.

"Oh, thanks," Skylar said, and before she could add to it, Abby took her hands, turned her, and planted a soft kiss on her lips.

"Don't be a stranger," Abby said. "Okay?"

Skylar's chest was aflutter. She'd mostly dated guys lately, but that kiss felt all the way right. "Of course. Yes."

Abby gave a curt nod and spun on her heels to head back inside.

Skylar watched her go through the glass doors, and once Abby reached the elevator past the lobby, she started toward the cube truck. It was a struggle to keep from skipping. She hoped her mother hadn't seen that kiss, she'd be all weird about it, making lovey-dovey jokes.

"Did I just see a smooch!" Hannah said the moment the van's shotgun door opened.

"Take a trip," Skylar said, blushing again.

"I am already, and so are you."

Skylar thought of Abby laughing about the cube truck and looked around the cab. There was room for all three, sure, but only two seats. In between was a hard plastic cooler full of who knew what.

"How are we all fitting in here?" Skylar said.

Hanna glanced over her shoulder to the cube and then

darted her eyes to the cooler. "Sorry, your brother's too big to sit on the cooler, and I have to drive."

Skylar huffed. They had the truck for a week and would rent a storage unit wherever they found what they were looking for if they couldn't move in right away. The hope was that they wouldn't have to stay in a hotel for more than a week.

"Say, let's get a pizza to eat on the way to getting your brother?" Hannah said.

Skylar opened her mouth to bemoan the plan but bit it down. Her mother was trying to look calm and happy, but it was obvious she was tired and not exactly thrilled about leaving the city, and perhaps even nervous about driving. "Sure," she said instead, adding, "When was the last time you drove something this big?"

Hannah whistled. "Never. I haven't driven anything but City Go cars in the last decade."

"So…pizza as a last meal then."

"Very funny…but maybe," Hannah said, making a face of mock terror, likely hiding the bit of real terror she surely harbored as she hit her blinker and pulled back into the heavy afternoon traffic.

THREE

Damp all over, face red, muscles achy, Gabe Laurie bent forward to jimmy his feet into his Nikes. Most of the guys were still screwing around in the showers, some not even in yet, but Gabe saw his mother and sister eating pizza on the sideline of the field while the team practiced and didn't want to make them wait. Especially not today.

The city was in a state of perpetual encroaching, rezoning anywhere they wanted, everywhere but a few select green spaces. Without green spaces, Vancouver would never coax the Olympics back, or the FIFA World Cup to town. It would never be about the locals, just how much more the local billionaires could hoard.

"Is tonight your last night?"

Gabe glanced over to Connor Plimpton, standing in a towel. He'd gone over all this; he'd still be around plenty, and he wasn't skipping out on the team—they were scheduled to participate in three off-season, U18 tournaments in the coming month and Gabe was going to be ready to play. The coach had set everything up when it came to off-season competition, stating to the guys that his biggest hope was to get scholarships for their best, but everyone knew the man simply loved winning. Though Gabe would take any scholarship he might earn.

"Last night was. Leaving right now," Gabe said and then pushed to stand.

"Oh, wild, well, the guys and I, we all got together to give you a gift," Connor said.

Eight young men rushed from the steamy shower, their feet slapping on the cold stone floor. They were naked and waggling themselves. Connor dropped his towel and waggled along. Gabe spun and sprinted away, knowing they'd charge at him the moment the fleshy clapping ceased. He reached the door just as Connor's hand grasped his shoulder, but Gabe had been anticipating this—or at least something along these lines—and rolled downward, lifting Conner from his feet as he swung open the door.

The hallway was empty but for two ESL students who had summer classes. Gabe continued running while Connor screamed and shouted for mercy. The ESL students backed up against a wall, wide-eyed, mouths agape. Gabe dropped Connor to the floor with a hearty, damp smack.

"See you next week!" Gabe continued forward while Connor covered himself, scrambling back toward the locker room, past the tittering ESL students. Two of the other guys had grabbed towels and stood sopping and laughing in the hallway next to the locker room door, shoving Connor so he couldn't get inside.

Outside, Gabe slowed, squinting into the sun. A cross-country running team was using the track and moving, more or less, in a pack. Once they'd gone by, he jogged onto the lush green of the field. New sweat was already beginning to prickle at the lingering dampness from the shower. At the center of the field, a girls' rugby team was stretching at the instruction of the nine/ten gym teacher who was barking orders in her school athletic uniform, despite that this was a community team. Gabe side-eyed the girls, looking for anyone he thought cute, but did not lose pace. He reached the fence on the opposite side of the field and jumped it with only a slight deviation to his stride. From ten feet away, he could see his sister's eye roll. They were sitting on collapsible camping chairs with a Panago Pizza box on a cooler between them.

"Hey," Gabe said and flipped back the lid. The box was empty.

"Hey," Hannah said, rising to her feet.

"What's this?" Gabe said, gesturing to the greasy stain, proof that the pizza had been there but was now gone.

Skylar stood and folded her chair, one-handedly; the other hand held a can of Dr. Pepper. She lifted the chair and Hannah accepted it. Skylar then grabbed the cooler and pizza box.

"Ease your jets, there's a whole 'nother pizza in the truck," Hannah said and started around back to stow the chairs behind the big, roll-up door.

Gabe watched his mother and then hurried up behind Skylar as she stuffed the pizza box into a trashcan. He grabbed her shoulder before she had a chance to make for the shotgun door.

"Did Dad text you?" he whispered.

Skylar scrunched her mouth to the left side of her face. "Yeah. 'Watch out for strangers, I'm serious;' what the hell does that mean?"

At the back, Hannah slammed the roll-up door closed, the sound something akin to a skateboarder nailing a wall. A couple pigeons looked their way, as if offended by any loud and grating sounds that marred all that nice greenery.

"You think he's in trouble again?" Gabe said.

After a huff, Skylar went and hopped into the truck, holding the cooler before her. She moved the second pizza box from the floor to the dash. The truck truly wasn't built for three riders up front. She fussed for a moment with the cooler before sitting down on it. Her eyes barely came above the dash, making her look childish between the captain's chairs in the cab. Gabe trailed after her and climbed in, immediately snatching at the warm pizza box.

"There's a Mountain Dew somewhere," Hannah said after getting behind the wheel. She put on her seatbelt and then looked down at Skylar. "If I crash, hold on."

"Take a trip," Skylar said, flipping the cooler lid enough to withdraw the promised Mountain Dew.

"Any dip?" Gabe said.

Skylar pointed as she sat back down and Gabe located the dip within the deep, deep cupholder. He set the dip inside the box after pulling the lid back. Within a few seconds, half the first slice was gone. Hannah pulled out of the lot and onto the street. Gabe cracked the Mountain Dew and sipped between big bites. City driving was tight and remained so until they hit the first provincial park. In front of them, a little Mazda convertible had a middle-aged woman behind the wheel with what appeared to be a teenager draped over her, rubbing her bare thigh up a skirt. The truck provided a new and unwelcome angle to such things.

"Gross," Hannah said.

"What?" Skylar said, too low to see.

Long before they got to the edge of the city, Gabe had eaten eight of twelve slices.

"Maybe save us a snack," Skylar said.

Gabe belched a great, barking release in response.

"Gross," Hannah said, again.

They got stuck at a red light in two lanes of northbound traffic—two lanes of southbound just across the yellow line. From behind, the great roar of two gasoline powered Harley Davidson motorcycles slipped between the deadlocked vehicles and did not stop until they hit the white line some twenty or so car lengths ahead. Harley Davidson branded gasoline motorcycles had become twice the eye-roll they'd been when gasoline vehicles were the norm. They were loud, they were gaudy, and the people who rode them appeared to have issues with insecurity, or at very least, they hated the planet. *Look at me!* these vehicles screamed. Though it was rare nowadays, occasionally biker gang violence and organized crime hit the headlines.

"When are we supposed to get to Whistler?" Gabe said as he tapped his index finger along to the latest Billie Eilish track coming through the tinny speakers of the cube truck.

"We're looking at a place in Garibaldi first, though I don't think it's in the budget. Mostly we just need to park at a power station for twenty minutes," Hannah said, leaned forward over the wheel, looking a bit stressed.

"We're not getting in Whistler, though? You said that," Skylar said.

"No, but there's a ton of new developments between Whistler and Pemberton. It's not like in Vancouver, either. The apartments are a little bigger. Plus, they're all next to dedicated forest, so lots of wildlife and whatnot. It should be peaceful…the tradeoff for being so far from everything," Hannah said, eyes pinned to the road, despite that they were moving about 5 MPH.

"There was a lady in the elevator who is going to be a tree-keeper," Skylar said. "Apparently you need to go to college for that job."

"They just want everybody to go to college," Gabe said, looking out the window at a bag lady pushing a shopping cart loaded with dirty old shoes. "I bet even that old woman went to college."

Hannah and Skylar both looked. Skylar kept looking long after Hannah's attention returned to the road.

"Probably she's got a PHD," Skylar said.

"In what?" Gabe said.

"Orthopedics?" Skylar said.

Hannah barked a single, overwrought laugh.

"Maybe she's a plastic surgeon for homeless people," Gabe said.

"Maybe she's a vet for stray cats."

"Maybe she's—"

Hannah interrupted the banter with, "Maybe life isn't fair and you two ought to remember when you were much younger. Imagine if we'd been kicked out of our home *without* a juicy check, imagine if we'd been kicked out back when you were little. I'd a been pushing you two in a shopping cart like that lady with her shoe collection."

Skylar rolled her eyes, getting her head and neck into the show of it. Gabe said and did nothing in response, instead let his eyes fall to the next homeless person, the one after that, the one following, and so on. He'd never once imagined himself in a situation so hapless and doing so was a touch unwelcome.

FOUR

The place in Garibaldi was a slum. The town itself hadn't yet been overrun by developers, but nothing much was up for rent because nothing had been upscaled in the way every building had been in Vancouver. Everywhere they looked—while they searched out a vacant charging station—were homes and apartment buildings with boarded windows and caving, mossy roofs. Long-term investors holding the properties until there was absolutely nothing left in Vancouver or its suburbs, which would then drive up the values. Otherwise, the town was nice thanks to the government regulated forest land and green spaces that were thick with wildflowers and the steady buzz of a thriving bee population.

Finally, a charging space opened up at a station across the street from a DQ—the building was old enough that the ghost of the words Dairy Queen remained like a dark aura, a memory of the world before lactose became a four-letter word. Hannah used her phone to place their order and pay. By the time they locked up the truck and the orange hand became a white walking figure, the food was ready. They accepted the trey and then stepped out to sit at a stone picnic table.

Hannah studied her Blizzard. "My mother was furious when they stopped using cow milk—"

Four gasoline-powered Harley Davidson motorcycles revved from the DQ lot around the side. It was impossible to tell if two of this foursome included the two from earlier. All four bikers had long greying beards, sunglasses, and big middles. They wore jeans and leather vests. Bandanas tied around their heads kept their long, scraggly hair out of their faces.

"Abso' baby peens," Gabe said, as he cut at the

banana in his sundae with the edge of his paper spoon.

Hannah snorted at this. "Insecure men, since the beginning of time, have tried to pass off exterior power with personal power. Same way all those rappers you like wear fake gold and diamonds and spend all their money buying Louis Vuitton belt buckles."

"LV's out," Skylar said around a creamy mouthful. "All about Prada this year for the uber staked."

"Same thing," Hannah said. "Even when I was young; all the same thing."

The Harleys seemed to have no business in DQ, or at the establishments surrounding it, or above it, and rolled away without dismounting from their bikes. Skylar squinted at this and then glanced at Gabe. He wasn't paying attention, so she said nothing. Probably one thing had nothing to do with the other, had nothing to do with their father's text messages.

It was 5:30 PM by the time they climbed into the rental and were back on the road, heading toward Whistler. The traffic was dense but moving. Next to the highway, amid the thick, thick foliage of thirteen-year-old trees, trains zoomed north and south in turn. Public transit was significantly quicker than private means until north of Whistler.

The real estate agent in Pemberton was busy until 8:00 PM, but said she was happy to show any vacant properties as late as was necessary. Skylar and Gabe listened to their mother while she spoke with her phone on speaker. When Hannah hung up, she looked at her kids, offering an exhausted smirk.

"Guess we should check in to our hotel," Hannah said.

They rolled another five minutes before reaching one of their destinations. Hannah pulled into the parking lot of the Best Western. It had about thirty floors that rose like Jack's bean stock amid all the relatively youthful trees surrounding the property. Beyond was the great mountain range that had supported the community since its inception.

"We're not staying, though?" Skylar said.

Hannah shook her head gently. "I'll fall asleep. We should go for a walk."

"I have to take a dump first," Gabe said before he kicked open the shotgun door.

Skylar pulled a face, though she'd be using the washroom right behind him. She and Gabe followed Hannah around back where she removed the padlock from the rolling door. Next to the collapsible chairs was a large suitcase that they'd packed together the night before. Out on the street, the Harley bikes appeared, rolling slowly. Each head of the foursome craned to look into the Best Western parking lot. An image of her father's text message flashed onto her mind.

Watch out for strangers I'm serious

She shook her head. She was being paranoid. This was a tourist town and what better place for middle-aged men to show off their specialty machines?

A young woman with terrible acne was manning the check-in desk. She wore the pleasant blouse and vest combination most hotels supplied as a uniform, and her hair was neat, held tight in a bun at the back of her head. Her smile was business, her voice matching. Skylar instantly felt sorry for her. When Skylar was twelve and puberty had begun to dig its claws, she'd broken out. It wasn't nearly as bad as this girl at the desk, but it felt like it. It felt like the end of the world. She'd cried and cried on her mother's lap after a rough day at school when a skinny little boy asked if she was trying to grow a tomato farm. Her mother had stroked her hair and promised it was all short-term. And it had been, within six months her chemicals had rebalanced, and she was down to here and there pimples; a perfectly reasonable, manageable sum. Gabe had never really had that problem, or any problems.

The loud revving of engines cut into her reverie and she turned to look through the glass lobby doors. The motorcycles roared by, one after the other, flashing black and orange. She looked at her mother and then to her brother. Her mother was busy, but her brother had noticed.

"Hey," Skylar said, then nodded over her shoulder as she took a step in reverse. "Did you actually text Dad back?"

The man had been on the path to reconnection for the last few years. Skylar wasn't moved by his plight or his promises that all the stupid stuff was in his past— Hannah had told them all about their father. Gabe was moved, at least a little bit.

"Yeah. I asked what he meant and he asked what we were doing tonight instead of answering my question," Gabe whispered.

"What'd you say?"

"Said we were going up to Pemberton to look at houses."

Skylar waited a few ticks and then said, "And what?"

"He just said that was good; when I asked him why, he didn't answer. I've texted him a few times since. Nothing."

"Ready?" Hannah said, yawning through the word as she held up a keycard.

Together they crossed the lobby to the wall of stainless-steel elevator doors. The stereo overhead piped in a soft instrumental tune. A hint of flower scent played upon the recycled air. A set of doors opened and a quintetof men, pale with close-cropped beards, wearing thobes and kaffiyehs, stepped in with them. Their heavy perfume remained in the car long after the men departed as the Laurie family continued up to the twentieth floor.

FIVE

Sheldon Finkelstein came to slowly, groggily, all alone. That was bad. The pattering he'd heard earlier had ceased, and that was good. The pain had become a dull throb, and that was good, too. He was woozy and weak, and that was bad, bad, bad. He tugged at the duct tape holding his arms to the chair. The men had first decided they were done listening to his bullshit around lunchtime and had then taped him to the chair. It only got worse for Sheldon from there.

The sweat had loosened the hold some when the tin snips had come out and then had carved through flesh, but not enough that he might free a hand. He'd lost two pinkies, two rings, and one middle finger. The pattering he'd heard had been his blood, once the gushing finally tapered off. The pain had been horrendous. It felt as if they'd been burning his flesh, on top of the marrow-deep agony of snapping bones. It had been so awful in fact that he couldn't keep his mouth shut about the check his ex-wife, Hannah, was about to receive—one his son, Gabe, had explained in detail. The only positive, the only hope, was that Sheldon had had an inkling about how the day might play out, and he had warned his kids to watch out for strangers...unfortunately, the passcode to his phone was the first thing he'd given up to Kristy Clarke's debt collectors.

Once a member of high society, Kristy Clarke had done one too many backroom real estate dealings that became public knowledge and had since completely lost interest in even pretending to be on the right side of the law. From real estate she took the natural step into money laundering. When sports gambling was legalized beyond the confines of the track and the casino, she got into fixing matches. A brief prison stint only hardened her further—despite her stay being in a federal facility and her cellmate being in on conspiracy to commit tax fraud, which made up about half the convicts on her block. She moved into drugs and was working alongside the Sun Yee On triad to give British Columbia all the opioids they'd ever need. This created a demand for muscle. She had many Sun Yee On members at her disposal, but preferred to toss any customs barriers out in order to deal with what she referred to as 'old stock Canadians,' when she hired the Black Teeth. They'd lost a few members recently to the prison system, but four wholly reliable, morally bankrupt bikers were all she required to do her dirtiest jobs. And to do them without complaints.

Sheldon squirmed and yanked at his wrists, trying to work the blood around the tape, slickening it. A steady moan played up from his chest and his breaths came out hot and ragged. He was in the sub-basement of a cruddy parking garage. Above him, outdated wires dangled like cobwebs. Ahead of him was a huge electrical panel on a cement wall. To his right was the washroom where he'd sent his final texts before his phone was stolen—the facilities within were surprisingly clean. To his left was another cement wall, its only notable attribute was a blood splash that had been there when he'd arrived. The art of the warning.

"Come on, you bitch," Sheldon groaned.

He was a chubby man with curly hair and a head full of bad decisions. He was tall, but weak. All his life, he'd been a man of many, many words. Talking had done him well in his youth, but once he got older, so did the people he was trying to charm. Generally speaking, these people had ceased falling for his bullshit more than a decade ago, and still, it was what he knew and change like that, a personality change, was more effort than he'd ever put into anything.

"Let go, you bugger," he said through gritted teeth as he shook and reefed against the tight and sticky hold.

A sudden jolt of pain had his head swimmy and his vision browning toward oblivion. Unwittingly, he ceased his effort to struggle free and sagged in the old wooden chair like a boxer on a stool unwilling to face the next round.

When the world returned to him, he had no idea of how much time had passed, or how much blood he'd lost. It certainly felt like a lot of blood.

"All right. All right," he mumbled. "Old Shelly's do for a W."

The blood had crusted and began crumbling at his resumed efforts. His hands weren't budging, and he leaned forward to see if there was something he was missing—aside, of course, from his fingers, those were on the floor by his feet. The different movement shifted the tape and fresh pain screamed through his nerves. Saliva dangled from his puffy lips as he huffed and moaned against the agony. He fought to keep focus, scanning everything for an answer. There was zero doubt in his mind that others had died down here, so there had to be something.

Tape encircled his ankles as well, though they'd done the right one last and hung on by its end, hanging the stiff cardboard roll like a limp flag on a pole. Perhaps they'd run out before perfecting the job. He sat back and started bouncing his knee, attempting to kick out. Nothing doing. He stopped a moment, took a deep breath, and then started shimmying left to right while lifting with his toes.

"Rip, you bitch," he said, sweat oozing from every pore. His shirt was sopping. Salt stung at his eyes. His mouth tasted of copper. "Rip, you troll!"

It did rip then, and his leg shot out sideways hard

enough to sting his hip. His hip hadn't been injured but being 48 was enough of a reason for his body to hurt at simple, vigorous motions. He yanked his leg back and stiffened until the overexerted muscle ceased its whale song.

"Okay," he said after a minute or more. "Okay."

With his free heel he began to push against the taut tape of the other leg. He had on newish loafers with good, stiff heels. They'd been designed to mimic much, much nicer shoes. That stiff plastic made to look like hardwood or cork tore into the tape. Sheldon grinned a mouth full of pink teeth and began kicking frantically, forward this time and with the other foot. The tape gave a great squelch, and his other foot was halfway free.

"Let! Go!"

He kicked and kicked and kicked, and finally, his legs were no longer fastened to the chair. He sat there, catching his breath, imagining the door opening and Kristy Clarke's men coming back a moment before he'd saved himself. An ugly thought. One bad enough to give his inner engine a little more gasoline.

He pushed to stand and began walking toward that bloodstained wall. The motions of his actions were odd and took time getting used to. Bent forward, he swung his back end around like a cat in heat. The heavy chair sapped his energy quickly. He groaned and moaned, smashing the legs. It wasn't working. He flopped down heavily.

A crack rang out.

"That's how you want it?" he said and popped to his feet and then dropped back hard, nearly hard enough to topple him in reverse. "Careful, don't want to be a turtle."

He stood and this time, instead of simply launching back, he jumped. His legs went out as straight as they could. The chair cracked thunderously in the quiet space.

There was a wobble beneath him. He stooped again, leapt, and kicked out his legs to land heavily. The wood broke under his weight. One of the spindles jabbed into his lower back and he squirmed around to relent this fresh trouble. After it was done, his arms remained stuck.

"Let me go!" he said.

Bent forward and pushing with all he had, coming up like the Incredible Hulk, the heavily cracked wood splintered out behind him. His arms were free enough to move, though still both had heavy chunks clinging to them. He got to his feet again and this time ran for the door, knowing it would be locked.

When he was a boy, his parents had locked him in the fruit cellar for many hours at a time. They'd used a chair on the outside of the door, and though he'd never wanted to garner attention by smashing at the door, he'd tried endlessly to weasel his way out. Never once did he sit and really consider how his thefts hurt shop owners and classmates, which was the point of this breed of punishment when sending him to temple had failed to produce results—it had instead given him new grounds for disruption. His parents had had to lock him down there, his silver tongue was simply too hard to ignore. Now, however, his tongue would do him no good against the deadbolt.

He grabbed the handle and spun, yanking as he did— his grip slipped and the ghosts of his missing fingers screamed for mercy. He flew backward, unready for the door to cooperate, but remained upright. Blink, blink, blinking and breathing heavily at the agony of the missing digits that had rubbed against the brushed steel of the doorknob, he charged ahead, certain the universe would reverse this misplaced luck, but that door remained open. He made it into another cement room with a steel staircase that had only one direction.

Up. There was a door at the top and that familiar fear came back, as did a warning that uncareful grabbing was going to be big trouble. Gently, he used his left and the three remaining fingers thereon, to turn the filthy handle. It hurt, but it wasn't the unholy war cry he'd felt upon opening the door into the stairwell. The door opened onto a parking garage packed with dusty automobiles that appeared as if they hadn't moved in years. Also, not five feet from the door was the sedan with the roomy trunk that had brought him here—Harley Davidson motorcycles weren't all that conducive to kidnapping. It was an older Tesla. The wheels bowed subtly outward at the weight and its poor design.

Finding two unlocked doors had Sheldon suddenly feeling that the abrupt, abnormal good luck might be with him yet.

"Can he go three for three?" he said and pulled at the Tesla handle.

Locked.

"Damn."

He turned just shy of a full circle before discovering the unmistakable stainless-steel doors of an elevator. They were dusty as the worst of the vehicles, and a great dent marred the right-side panel. That didn't matter, so long as it went upward.

Staggering, woozy once again, Sheldon crossed the quiet parking area and pressed the call button. He leaned with his warm forehead against the cool wall. It came to him then that he'd told those maniacs where his children were likely going to be. Telling them where Hannah was, that didn't bother him so much, but the kids. What kind of sad excuse for a father would do that?

The elevator doors opened, and he stepped inside. He tapped a grimy button with a G on it and the doors closed. Within seconds, the doors opened, and he looked out at a hallway with endless stalls on either side. He was in one of those internet cafes that people had taken to living in—he'd spent more than a few nights in them himself. A boy and a girl walked by to get a cup of ramen from a machine. They were young and disheveled, of West Asian descent, perhaps North African, but they made him think of Skylar and Gabe in a way that cut him deep.

"It's your screwup, not theirs."

For the first time in a very long time, Sheldon had a completely selfless thought. He had to go north. He had to right this wrong. To hell with his debt to that greedy psycho, Kristy Clarke. To hell with amoral junkie bikers. To hell with tomorrow, he had to help them today. Sheldon Finkelstein had to make this right if it was the last thing he did with his miserable life.

Running on fumes, he made his way to the busy street and the throngs of people ignoring how dirty and bloody he was. He scanned the surroundings to understand exactly where he stood. Vancouver was his city and getting his bearings shouldn't take more than one, two, three seconds…once he had it, he started moving again, meandering through the crowd of people staring at phones and holo tablets. After passing through the busiest section of the block, he stepped over a short fence and into a parking lot.

The bikers had left him his wallet—they had however taken his last hundred bucks cash—and from it he produced his ID card. He scanned it at the City Car terminal and then pressed an index finger to the pad. The information matched. He went with the first option and started an open tab. Come tax season, they'd nail him for this rental—taking a City Car to Pemberton would cost a small fortune. If he survived that long, he'd be happy pay the toll.

"No," he said. "You won't be happy, but you'll do it…maybe."

He got behind the wheel and put two locations into the autopilot GPS. He needed food first of all, and located a Vera's Burger Shack along the way to Pemberton—it wouldn't do to sidetrack far, but he needed fuel for this fight. The real struggle would be eating one of their wondrously huge burgers with only five fingers. The car started rolling. Sheldon tried to imagine how he'd stop the leather-clad nightmares but decided that was a problem for later. He had to get to his family first.

Besides, he was feeling lucky, and perhaps the universe would provide an unexpected doorway to success.

SIX

Hannah had fallen asleep almost instantly upon entering the room, and only awoke when Gabe began shaking her. She sat up, stiffly, bending at the hips and bringing her abdomen forward, something like a vampire rising to begin the night's events. It took a moment for her to understand that she was in the hotel room and had fallen asleep. She wrinkled her nose at the scent lingering in the little bathroom—the room itself was barely large enough for two twin beds and a cot on rollers.

"What time is it?" Hannah said.

"Quarter after seven," Gabe said.

He sat on the other bed. Skylar stood by a window that did not open more than a crack. She pulled aside the curtain and leaned closer to the glass, as if trying to see around a corner, studying something below.

"Guess we'd best boogie," Hannah said and shimmied down to the end of the bed until her feet touched the floor.

Standing out in that cold hallway with her kids, Hannah wished for *home* and her bed in her familiar room. She wished nothing had to change and she could simply go on as she always had. Mostly, she wished and yearned for that sense of private, personal space.

Thoughts of Annette bounced into her head, and she forced herself to be grateful, as things could be much, much worse. Would Annette ever have a place to call her own again, or would she live the rest of her days in a cubicle that rented by the hour and smelled like boiled water and hot dust? The notion of it was enough to make her cringe, especially when she acknowledged how easily it might've been her.

"Damned Dìzhŭ Corp," she whispered and followed her kids to the elevator.

Skylar looked around the parking lot as soon as they stepped through the lobby doors, back into the late spring heat. The scan was expansive, almost methodical, as if she expected to see something.

"What?" Hannah said.

Skylar looked at Gabe and then to her mother. She sighed. "Dad sent these cryptic texts about strangers. I'm guessing he did something stupid and…" She trailed off, no need to elaborate further.

Gabe frowned at his sister.

"What?" Skylar said. "We've seen those bikers three times, and Dad did say to watch out."

Gabe faced forward and stomped toward the box truck, as if this was some grand betrayal.

Hannah could only roll her eyes at the kids. Anything their father said had to be about 95% bullshit. The man never changed. It was a shame it took her so long to acknowledge this, and even longer for her to come to accept that she wasn't going to fix him. On the bright side, he had provided half the genetics of two great kids and had only been an occasional bother since she sent him packing oh so many years ago. The only thing that would've been better was if he'd died sometime through the years; be out of all their lives in that respectable way death offered that mere absence did not. The cherry would be if he'd at some point purchased a life insurance policy, though the notion of his thinking that much of them over his current financial needs was laughable.

They climbed into the rental, Skylar again riding low on the cooler and looking none too pleased about it. The traffic was moderate, but slow-moving. Whistler was a beautiful place with a ton to see. The buildings were lush and fanciful, sure, but beyond, the mountains stretched into the clouds, their white caps above charcoal bases were stark and dynamic. The foliage worked opposite to the mountains—dark green below and light above in the blue, blue sky. That check from the Dìzhǔ Corporation wouldn't put a dent in anywhere but bachelor housing in Banff. It had always been outrageous—not as bad as Vancouver, but for a place away from the coast with only tourist industry money, it was miles more than the surrounding areas.

About a decade earlier they'd plowed over the final small dwellings and comparatively cheap apartments in Banff, and the *unskilled* labor moved into apartments beneath the new hotels like rats in sewer tunnels. No matter how awful that sounded, at least Whistler had banned the 24-hour internet cafes that had people living in cost-effective digital realities—like Annette. Hannah shivered, shaking away Annette's situation from the forefront of her mind.

Tourists in rental cars. Tourists on buses. Tourists crossing streets, willy-nilly. Everyone was looking at something. The sun had become a hot pink ball behind the grand mountain range, giving the stone peaks and valleys a fantastical aura.

"If we have to look at something like that every night, I guess it won't be all bad," Hannah said.

Gabe and Skylar both looked up from their phones. But only for a glance.

"Probably it's that color because of pollution," Skylar said, eyes again stuck to her device.

Hannah frowned but reached into the dash console for her own phone as they waited at a red light. She quickly checked for notifications—there were six, but nothing demanding—and then began the GPS routing she'd pulled up the night prior.

"Drive thirty-four kilometers. Take a right on Chasburn Avenue," said the slightly robotic voice from the phone's little speaker.

The front right wheel humped over the lip of the asphalt and onto the gravel shoulder. Hannah gasped and yanked the wheel, overcorrecting. The rubber squealed and she yanked back right. The vehicle in sudden peril, threatening to tip, Skylar grabbed onto stiff seatbelt couplers rising from the floor. Hannah attempted to give the wheel a third yank, but the emergency system had taken over to keep her from rolling the truck. Huffing, heart going about 200 beats per minute, she turned the wheel slightly to put them safely back onto their side of the road once the vehicle had settled. Both kids were staring at her, eyes agape.

"We're okay," Hannah said. Her hands were gripped so tightly they looked a bit like strawberry swirl yogurt—intensely white in most places with deep red patches throughout. "Eyes on the prize."

"If we crash, I'm probably dead," Skylar said, serious as brimstone in a church sermon. "I'll never go to college."

Hannah leaned in closer to the steering wheel. "We're fine. Now, shush, I'm concentrating."

Gabe reached over and killed the radio—it had been on low as it was. "You got this," he said.

"She just about crashed us!" Skylar said, growing more excited with the passing seconds. "Jesus, what if we'd crashed?" She began looking around the cab of the truck. There was a black ratchet strap beneath the seat. "I'm not dying before I go to college."

"Will you shut up! Nobody's dying and we're not going to crash!" Hannah said, certain the very opposite was about to happen. Adrenaline had her body thrumming and yet emptied from the center out. She was but a visage of herself, feeling weak and shaky and wholly unequipped to be piloting such a huge machine.

"What are you doing?" Gabe said.

Skylar was fidgeting with the ratchet strap. "Going to

make myself a seatbelt so that when Mom ditches this—"

"I'm not ditching anything!" Hannah shouted.

Near-silence filled the cab immediately after the scolding. The electric engine rolled them along almost soundlessly. The cab's air-conditioning sang a subtle hum. Their breaths came out ragged and harsh, though hardly loud enough to note.

In the distance, though closing in on them quickly, came the roaring of gasoline-powered motorcycle engines. Hannah looked in her side mirror, her eyes darting back and forth. Now she was getting as paranoid as the kids about Sheldon and his endless mistakes. Was it possible that one of those mistakes might cause serious damage to her, and more importantly, the kids?

"Worry about driving," she mouthed.

1999 – 48 YEARS AGO

"Come on, you don't want to be down there with the sheeple when the computers crash," Joel Johansson said as he led the trio onto a slim no winter maintenance road. They were wearing snowshoes and lugging huge packs on their backs, leaving behind their vehicle just off the highway. It had been obvious to all three that December 31st, 1999, was going to be the final day of this civilization; there'd be nothing but chaos and violence moving forward. They'd held discussions for months leading up on where to go and how to get there, but Joel was the only one of the threesome who knew the exact spot to go in order to survive until the bedlam cleared.

His father had told him of this family of weirdos and their bunker, just south of Pemberton. Before sunrise on New Year's morning, the nukes would rain unholy terror upon the world as the computers crashed, and only people hiding in bunkers had any chance at all.

"It's not that far," Joel said, though he wasn't entirely certain as he'd never seen the place.

The ruined and scavenged house was no surprise, but the decently kempt cottage in the backyard on the hill *was* a surprise. Someone had been there after what his father had told him had gone on, thankfully, nobody dug up or removed a bunker, and while the cottage was in okay shape, it certainly hadn't been lived in recently.

The trio hurried on top of the crunchy snow, their breaths pluming out in white clouds that lingered in the stilled atmosphere. Joel glanced back at his compatriots and then tried the door handle. Unlocked. They entered without issue, discovering the interior intact.

"Think the bunker's in here?" Corina said. She was

the crux that held the love triangle together.

"Either way we have to—" Buck began but was interrupted by Joel.

"The bunker is on the hill. My dad told me so. He knew the guy who put in the lines that ran to creek generators. There has to be floor access. This cabin was built later, on top. Somewhere around here's floor access." Joel scanned the floor from the doorway as he spoke.

Corina huffed. "You hope so. No way we find it out there under all that snow."

It seemed none had considered the snow in regard to finding something underground. Buck got big eyes and looked at Corina. Joel ignored them as he bent over and unlatched the rubber straps of his aluminum snowshoes. He set them outside the door, standing them against the wall. The others followed suit.

It took about a minute to fully adjust to the dimness within the cottage. It was sparsely furnished and it appeared that, in the warmer months, spiders ruled the roost. Thick grey cobwebs draped down from every surface, drab and lifeless as moth-eaten silk.

"Feels like we're in a haunted house," Corina said. Before she'd followed her boyfriends to an escape van fueled by paranoia, she'd been taking strides toward achieving an MFA in English. She wanted to be a writer. Twelve rejection slips on her first three stories made it easier to skip out on school, her debts, and her undoubtedly disappointed parents. "If you think I'm holding your hand, it's actually a ghost," she added, though none got the reference.

"What?" Buck said, kneeling before a greasy kerosene heater.

"Just a joke," Corina said, she reached up and tried a light switch on the wall. Nothing. She flicked it five times in rapid succession.

Joel stamped his boot on the wooden floor. It sounded hollow, but there was also a metallic rattle. "Shh, listen." He stamped again. The rattle was the same, like a chaser after the hollow thud of the wood. He stamped once more to narrow the sound.

"Over there," Corina said, pointing with her mittened hand.

In the kitchen, just past a dining table, was a large swatch of rug, ruffled and blocking the view of the floor behind it until standing directly above it. Joel grinned and knelt. He grabbed the steel ring—almost certainly the source of the rattle—and swung it upward. Beneath was a hatch, a handwheel. It was thick steel, something like a body might expect to see on a submarine though the door itself was much more than any expectations or daydream he'd had when he'd thought about locating it. Really, it was massive, about big enough to cart a couch through. He turned the wheel, the steel creaking theatrically. The door had hydraulic arms that bore most of the weight. The air was surprisingly fresh, and warm.

"Wow," Corina said.

The opening led down a smooth and steep ramp. There was light down there, meaning power, meaning the generators had to still be working.

"It's here. It's really here," Joel said, as if his deceased father's information might not be trustworthy.

On the underside of the wooden door above the hatch was an arm on a hinge. Joel stretched it out and leaned it on a frame ledge beneath. A sweet smell wafted up from the hole, accompanying the freshness. It almost felt as if they were discovering a utopia rather than a fallout shelter.

"Must be something growing down there…greenhouse?" Corina said. She and Buck stood on either side of Joel.

"There's still power down there, at least," Buck said.

"That was my big concern. It'll be off the grid, too, like you said."

Joel was nodding absently as he took the first steps down the slick wooden ramp. "Must've made it easier to move furniture," he said. The sweet smell grew thicker with each step, as did the warmth. It had a balmy quality to it. "Must've left a heater on; unless there is a greenhouse, perhaps growing out of control."

Joel reached the bottom and paused there, trying to understand what he saw. The others came down behind him and then stopped just as he had. The shelves to their sides were loaded with useful looking stuff, though useless to general survival. Before them was an ominous foggy wall, the now obvious source of the light and the heat. Around the fog was thick steel, wires streaming from it like hair. Each wire had a tab of masking tape on it with sharp black writing.

"That a tunnel?" Buck said.

"How big is the bunker? Does it keep going?" Corina said.

Joel started forward. "Must," he said. "My dad said nothing about all this."

Corina stepped in behind him and Buck trailed after her. Like three recently unincorporated souls, they walked slowly toward the light. Corina bumped into Joel when she stepped blindly into the fog. Buck managed to sidestep around both, despite not seeing the route.

So bright, they squinted. It wasn't another room in the bunker but a whole new world instead. A summery place with big trees, plants, and strange mushrooms, massive things. Joel continued forward, unzipping his parka as he went.

"What the fu—oog!" Joel got out.

About the size of a baby rhinoceros, a quadruped with sandy flesh barreled into his side with its incredible shell-like face. Joel pinwheeled through the air before coming to land in the sand dune immediately to their left. Buck looked at Corina and Corina looked at Buck. That beast was incredible, huge and fast, and so, so lumpy. It seemed as if bones jutted out everywhere beneath its tough flesh, though they didn't move when the beast moved.

"What the hell," Corina said, slack jawed as a cartoon yokel.

Armor, those protrusions were armor. The beast bucked and bounced playfully as it chased after Joel's tossed body.

"No!" Buck shouted and charged toward Joel.

The beast stopped dead and popped around, bouncing up from its tight little knees and landing on its grand trunk-like feet. The action was so juvenile it was impossible to deny the likelihood that this was a smaller version of something much bigger and nastier.

Corina, stuck in place, shocked into a statue, watched as the beast bent and leapt, pounding into Buck before landing on his stomach. The weight force was intense, launching his guts upward. His neck bulged like an overstuffed sausage, the skin tearing, blood splashing before oozing. His eyes bounced frantically around their sockets, disconnected from one another. His mouth vibrated, wide open and silent. Beneath, his pants had loaded with intestines from where they surged through his scrotum in a great piling coil. His testicles ruptured. His anus blew out like a waxy pink tail.

"Corina," Joel said from where he lay in the sand.

Sure, that was her name, but what was she going to do? There was no fixing this. Coming here had been a big damned mistake.

Shadows played down over the dune. The beast continued hopping and popping, turning Buck's corpse into a blood puddle. The shadow grew deeper, darker. Corina peeled her eyes from the carnage and looked to the incredible bird swooping overhead, dive-bombing toward the activity. Its taloned feet latched onto Joel's thigh, digging deep into the flesh. He wailed. The flying beast flipped him high in the air, where, once again, he pinwheeled. This time he had a momentarily softer landing, onto a tongue, between teeth. The flying beast's jaws closed around him. A great gush of blood splashed out.

A single drop of that hot, hot blood carried all the way to Corina, marking her forehead like a Bindi. The impact struck her like a taxi rolling at full speed. She staggered backward. But this was good; backward was the ticket.

She spun and ran, stumbling through the mist and tripping into the bunker. She landed hard on the cold floor. The dimness enveloped her, and she gulped a deep and thankful breath in relief.

Had all of that been real?

Were those dinosaurs?

Were Joel and Buck truly dead—

Through the mist, a long beak-like face appeared. It looked at Corina. She kicked out her left foot, striking the animal in the nose. She rolled over and backpedaled. That snout drew closer. She kicked again, this time it snapped at her, snatching her foot and dragging her back through the time portal.

It had been a frenzy after Dr. Pierre Racicot had gone through. Though more than 25 years had passed on one side, through the time portal, it had been but weeks. All within earshot had come to see what the upheaval had been about, and a few were rewarded with small but tasty meals of evolved flesh.

As Corina lay on her side, being devoured alive by the creature with the long snout and razor-sharp pebble teeth, she watched a painted turtle climb onto the top of the dune from the far side and then bury itself in the

WHERE THE DINOSAURS ROAM

sand. Her final thought was to wonder how the turtle managed to get a rope tied around its middle.

SEVEN

Gabe watched the side mirror with mounting dread. One of the bikers had zoomed up to about a car length from the cube truck and was reaching behind him into a saddle bag of some fashion. Once, two years ago or more, he and his father had gone to the hipster theater downtown for a double feature: *Satan's Sadists* and *The Wild Angels*. In both, the bikers were unflinching maniacs, and at the time, Gabe had hooted and laughed along with his father, but there was nothing funny about the idea that something like what those movies depicted happening in real life.

The man straightened, one arm by his side. He'd grabbed something; what it was that he retrieved, Gabe couldn't tell until the man rolled up close enough to kiss their bumper. His arm lifted and reared back. The spiked ball of the mace slammed into the cargo hold of the truck. Inside, it sounded like a shotgun blast.

"What the hell was that?" Hannah shouted, nearly bent over the steering wheel, her right foot easing off the gas pedal.

"Drive! Faster!" Gabe said.

"What is it?" Skylar said, still trying to figure out the ratchet strap to fasten herself in place.

"The bikers. It's like Dad said! It's like *Satan's Sadists!*" Gabe's entire face seemed to stretch, opening wide, wide, wide in terror.

"Who the hell are Satan's sadists?" Skylar shouted back, but Gabe didn't answer, his focus once again pinned to his side mirror.

A second biker had caught up, his engine growling in unison with the first, like a warning from Cerberus. The second biker swerved out into the now empty left lane.

He had a sawed-off, double-barrel shotgun in his right hand. He fired, taking Hannah's side mirror off in a cloud of plastic shrapnel, leaving behind a series of dangling wires. She screamed and jerked the wheel to her right and then overcorrected to her left. Before the emergency system had a chance to intervene, she'd knocked the shotgun wielding biker down, sent him tumbling into rolls while his bike slid in a celebration of sparks. The first one who'd closed in gave a single additional swing with his mace before slowing.

Instantly, the Harley growl lessened, playing away until it was nil, but Hannah kept her foot pinned. "Are they gone? Are they gone?" she said.

"They're back with the one you hit," Gabe said.

"Dammit," Skylar said, still trying—and failing—to get the strap to play out of the ratchet so that she could affix a makeshift seatbelt.

Ahead, the road curved. Hannah remained draped over the steering wheel, face as close to the windshield as was possible. Her foot was hard on the gas pedal.

"Mom!" Gabe shouted as the road bent harshly and Hannah did not react in time to the change.

The cube truck launched through a guardrail and down fifteen feet to a grassy ravine below. Gabe and his mother jerked against their belts while Skylar slammed into the ceiling, rolling before landing on her shoulder upon the dashboard. Glass shattered. Steel crunched. Air hissed. Plastic crumpled. The truck rolled only once before slamming into a tall spruce tree and coming to a dead stop. Hannah gasped. Gabe wheezed. Skylar lay silent, curled on her head. They remained unspeaking for about five seconds before the roar of motorcycles resumed, distant but approaching fast.

Gabe grabbed Skylar and shook her gently. Her body lolled and tipped to her left as her eyes fluttered open.

"Wake up," Gabe said.

"Don't move her!" Hanna said, tears streaming down her cheeks as she wrestled with a bent seatbelt buckle.

Skylar came suddenly conscious, and she screamed until it became a racking cough as she struggled to right herself. She jerked sideways onto Gabe. He held her tight as he could.

"Thank you," he said.

The motorcycles were close now. Too close.

"We have to move. Whatever your father did..." Hannah trailed. Her seatbelt had come open and she canted toward the middle of the truck while she tried to pull her body through the driver's window.

The tree they'd struck was more on the driver's side than the passenger's so Gabe pushed Skylar up so that she could climb out the front where the windshield had been. He followed her then, crawling into the pebbled glass and soft dirt beneath the big tree. She got to her feet and immediately swayed. Gabe popped up to his knees, arms out to steady her.

"Come on!" Hannah said, somewhere between a hiss and a yell as she tipped out and rolled to the dirt. "They're coming!"

The trio, moving just shy of a jog, pushed through the thick brush deeper into the forest. Those motorcycle engines echoed off trees and rocks, sounding as if coming from every direction. The strongest was directly behind them, so Gabe pulled his mother and sister to the right, trying to shift the route. The sun was all but down now and that was both good and bad. Darkness would hide them from the bikers, but also from anyone noticing the ruined guardrail and the crashed cube truck in the ravine below. They stumbled and bumbled, but they were finding deeper cover.

"Where are we going?" Hannah said, her breaths ragged and pained.

"Away," Gabe said, voice frantic but breathing

easily.

Skylar said nothing but the way she wheezed suggested she wouldn't be running for long. She pulled out her phone and the light was almost blinding.

"Get somewhere safe, first. They'll see the light," Hannah said.

"Where?" Gabe said.

Hannah didn't waste a beat and started away anew. Pushing along, moving toward the unknown. The motorcycle engines no longer growled, instead they purred, idling, suggesting they'd reached the cube truck. Suggesting the Laurie trio had to get moving or find somewhere safe to hunker down.

"Run," Hannah whispered, as if those machines were now on top of them.

"Look," Skylar said, leaned on a knee and pointing further to their right. Through the trees, the last rays of evening light glinted pinkly off something metallic. "See?"

"Wait here," Gabe said.

He took off, running low, eyes on his feet. He jumped, sidestepped, skipped, veered around trees, rocks, and undefinable masses in the deep shadows of the forest. So focused on his footfalls he ran into a rusty fence that bounced him like wrestling ring ropes. The toppers on the posts remained free of rust, little pink domes shining in the night thanks to the lingering light. Beyond, the trees cleared to reveal the wreckage of an old house and up on a hill was a small cottage that appeared to be intact. It was fully dark, but it gleamed like a promised land in the bleakness of the situation. Gabe turned back and burned toward his family.

The motorcycle engines were in motion again. They rolled away, sounding as if moving south. Gabe could hope against likelihood, but he wasn't willing to bet they were about to leave them alone. No way. Whatever their father had told these…Gabe got it then.

"Dad, no."

Gabe had been the one to make the first mistake. He'd told his father about moving, of course, but he'd also told him about the payout and the check they were to receive that very day. He told him about where they were going to look for housing. He gave his father a robbery roadmap. This being true, not for a second did he think his father was in on it. That did not mean he didn't know how weak-willed and selfish the man was.

"There's a cottage over there," he said once he reached Skylar and Hannah.

The motorcycle engines began playing closer, now from a different angle. Gabe gasped. If there was a cottage, then surely a path existed to it.

"We have to move fast. There's a fence," he whispered, his voice harsh as a smoker's cough.

At about half the speed Gabe had moved initially, the trio cut toward the fence. Skylar whined when she reached up to lace her fingers into the rusty metal. Gabe lifted at her thighs while Hannah climbed, clumsy but moving in the right direction. Once Skylar reached the top, Gabe scrambled up and over as if he'd done it a thousand times, touching down on the far side before his mother and sister had a chance to begin their descents. Arms up, he took much of Skylar's weight, lowering her slowly. Hannah got halfway down and dropped, landing on her heels and then butt.

"Ughhh," Hannah groaned through clenched teeth.

"You okay?" Gabe said—to both.

The motorcycle headlights burned through the trees, ominous, low-scale pyrotechnics. Gabe grabbed Skylar behind the knees. She latched onto his neck. He ran, Hannah did her best to keep up. They bypassed the ruined home, only slowing once the hill demanded they do so.

Hannah got to the door first and swung it open. Distantly, chains clanked against gravel. The sound was like a shovel into the dirt of their collective grave. Gabe set Skylar down and they entered the cottage. Hannah closed the door behind them, feeling for a lock and finding none. The space was almost full-dark, but across the room, rising from beneath the floor was a slight greenish glow.

"Where do we go?" Gabe said.

Hannah began to cross the room, bumping into furniture hidden by shadows. Skylar followed. Gabe gave a final look out a small window and then trailed.

"Down here," Hannah said. She reached back for Skylar's hand, and they descended the wide ramp. "Close the door behind us, Gabe."

He didn't need to be told. He pulled against the wooden door. It stuck, denying him. The motorcycles were right outside. Light shined into the cottage, revealing the prop arm. Gabe knocked it away and the door dropped. He stepped further down the ramp and pulled the heavy, heavy hatch door closed as well. It didn't appear to have a lock, but it did almost silence the motorcycle engines.

"What is that?" Skylar said.

Gabe turned and continued deeper into the bunker. His mother and sister were staring into the foggy green space. It smelled damp, earthy.

"Maybe there's a tunnel to a bog?" Hannah said. "Bogs are foggy from the water?"

Distantly, almost imperceptibly, boot-falls thudded against the floorboards. The trio looked to the ceiling. They waited, breaths bated, bodies stilled, hearts hammering.

"They're going to find us," Hannah said.

Skylar was the first to move. She looked at the foggy gateway and accepted its mystery as an offer.

"What if it goes to a bear's den, or something?" Gabe said, low.

"Better bears than bikers," Hannah said.

They continued then, toward the portal. On a shelf, about eye level, was a hatchet with a grey handle and red head. Gabe grabbed it and followed his sister and mother into the unknown.

EIGHT

Hannah sighed thankfully upon seeing an open sky above. The darkness was thick, but the temperature was warmer, which gave an excuse to the fog that had lingered in the strange gateway…though not why there was no fog now that they'd crossed through. Skylar stumbled once, and Hannah had to hold her steady. It hurt to see her daughter in pain, but this openness felt like an escape from much, much worse than whatever strains, bumps, or bruises Skylar was feeling.

"Watch yourself," Hannah whispered, seeing a rope between Skylar's feet, one end driven into the heavy sand. It was then that she noticed something peculiar. The moon was high and large, too high and too large, and the coloration of the sky was nothing like it had been. "Something's funny."

"We have to find somewhere to hide," Skylar said, holding her side.

The world looked so different from what they knew as normal. The mountains no longer loomed over them, but that had to be a trick of the light. Ahead was a skinny lake, or perhaps large pond—had the lake somehow gone unnoticed beyond the cabin? It seemed unlikely. There were trees and oddly shaped shrubs—they looked like massive mushrooms, but that didn't make any sense. They couldn't be mushrooms, right?

No matter the view, they got moving again, and at a pace a little quicker than a jog. All around them, though distantly, were animal sounds and rustling amid the foliage. Hannah and Gabe regularly stole peeks behind them to see if any man-shaped figures were on their trail, and the absence of engine sounds was a balm rubbed onto a huge chunk of the terror they'd felt.

This scene, along with the change in atmosphere, made Hannah think of her youth and camping with Sheldon—Shelly, as they'd all called him—and a group of friends. There was a cabin, but the owner didn't want them inside, instead, they pitched tents around a murky grey pond. Hannah and two other girls went with Rebecca Schubert, who was bringing along her boyfriend. Her boyfriend brought along three other boys, one being Shelly. It had been mid-August over in Banff. A hot and dry streak had forbidden them from having a campfire, so all night they danced around a lantern flashlight—fortunately, there'd been an outlet on the side of the house and the battery charger was quick enough to keep them lit. They had a wind-up radio and beer enough to last them a week if they didn't get fall down drunk every day—most days they had.

On the first night, all but Rebecca and her boyfriend slept in same-sex tents. By the following night, everyone had paired up. Hannah had counted herself lucky to match with Shelly rather than one of the others. He was funny, and knowledgeable, and had endless ideas. He had insane stories, adventures with the high school drama club, the summer he worked at an amusement park and had to wear different masks every day, and a teacher who eventually went on the run after robbing a bank. He talked and talked and talked until he slipped his tongue in her mouth. Given that there were only three tents, they ran through the dark forest, hand-in-hand, while Shelly looked for the perfect tree. According to him, if they didn't want to be eaten alive by a bear or black flies, they had to get high. "Then it won't matter that we're naked," he'd said. To which Hannah replied, "Oh, you think so?" A good tree eventually presented itself. They didn't get naked that night, but they'd spent hours straddling the huge branch and chatting about nothing much—they did get a chance to explore one another once on even ground, and as far as Hannah could figure, it was the weekend she'd conceived Skylar.

"We need to find a tree. We can watch from up high," Hannah said. "They won't think to look for us in the trees."

Skylar groaned. "I think I broke a rib." After a pause, she added, "Bit my tongue, too."

An intense manure scent bloomed around them, and Hannah instinctively veered them away. Any animal that produced a stink like that was an animal to avoid. It almost certainly had to be a bear. Bears were thick in the mountains near Banff and north, as well as the forested valleys below.

"Mom, what about that one?" Gabe pointed to a copse of tall, bone-like trees with thick grey limbs that began just a few feet from the ground.

"Yes," Hannah said, and they veered to their right, putting distance between themselves and the water, and the shit scent.

Gabe had to do most of the lifting for Skylar after she wrapped her arms and chest over the lowest limb. Skylar moaned and took deep, panting breaths. Hannah watched from the bottom, wincing with her daughter, until her children were two limbs up—about ten feet from the ground.

"Keep going. We need to be out of the sightline if they come through!" Hannah whisper yelled.

A little voice in her mind jabbed: 'Come through what?' That foggy doorway, gateway, whatever, had been strange, but not as strange as the change in atmosphere, temperature, and position of the moon. They'd come through something and weren't in Kansas anymore. She reached up and took hold of that lowest hanging branch. As she did, she stopped momentarily. A growling played through the night. At least they'd gotten a good head start.

All three held their breath, waiting, waiting, waiting for the Harley lights to cut through the shadows of the forest.

But that growl was not from an engine and was far enough away. Strange, and still, Hannah scrabbled up after her kids. Gabe had stopped on a deformed limp that had merged with another limb sometime in the tree's youth, creating a smooth, dusty basket. Skylar sat with her back against the trunk. Gabe sat cross-legged. Hannah finally worked her way up and thumped down heavily, letting her legs drape lazily over one side.

"Good. This'll do for a while," Hannah said.

Gabe leaned closer to his mother. "Something's funny here," he whispered.

Skylar had her shirt up and was trying to shine light from her cellphone onto the wound. It was ugly, already purple at the center of a great red lump of swelling. Gabe pulled out his phone then.

"No bars," he said.

Hannah's phone was in the truck, in her purse. She wondered if a real estate agent would be worried about a prospective client not showing up and doubted it. That kind of thing happened all the time. On the tail of the last, another thought struck: thankfully, she'd taken that massive check to the bank minutes after receiving it. Say a first responder found it and had sticky fingers, or a curious deer ate it, or one of the bikers…

Hannah closed her eyes, getting it fully. "You told your father about the check, didn't you?"

Gabe lowered his phone. "How could I…? It was just…just conversation."

Hannah huffed out a long and exasperated exhalation. "It's not your fault. You'll never see him for who he is. Took me years and he was around every day. That man would literally sell you into slavery if his back was against the wall."

Before Gabe or Skylar could add to the conversation, another distant growl cut through the night. This time there was no doubt of location: it had come directly from the area they had come from. With the sound came light. This growl was mechanical and all too familiar.

"They brought their bikes into the bunker?" Skylar said, whining it out.

Hannah turned from the direction of the noise and looked at her kids. "Exactly what did your father say?"

"Something about strangers, that's it," Skylar said.

Gabe brought the hatchet out from the back of his pants, as if it might stand a chance in hand-to-hand combat. It was almost enough for Hannah to let out a miserable laugh, but she swallowed it down. Perhaps that hatchet would save them somehow.

NINE

Sheldon awoke from a feverish dream. His shirt, which had dried and had gone crusty from all the blood and mucous that had oozed from his wounds, was once again damp, particularly beneath the collar and the moons of his breasts. He reached out for the steering wheel as he recognized the city of Whistler passing him by. The pain struck up from his missing digits like lightning through his nervous system. His entire body began to shake while the pain eased. Not far ahead was a high-rise tower with a bright red Shoppers Drug Mart shining onto the dim street below. He stabbed at the GPS twice and then used the voice command to redirect the autopilot.

"Stop at Shoppers Drug Mart." His voice was harsh, his throat ravaged by earlier screams.

The GPS instantly added the marker to the trip and the right turn signal began to flash as there was an open parking spot two buildings down from the drugstore. In the corner of the GPS monitor was the total fare cost thus far: $598. An unavoidable grimace flashed onto his face.

"Need to win the lottery by the time this thing's over," he said.

With a ginger effort and pinpoint precision, Sheldon opened the driver's door. Avoiding fresh pain was enough for him to heave a sigh as he climbed out, using his elbows instead of his hands to steady himself. With a swing of the hip, he bumped the door closed. A counter on the dash began—he had three hours before the vehicle would automatically return to one of the charging stations within the city limits of Vancouver, at his expense. He reached the automatic doors and had to wait as two elderly women with Hermès walkers and Gucci oxygen masks shuffled out of the way. Whistler was like a foreign country when compared to the inner-city lifestyles. These people were wearing and leaning on—and most likely had medical devices installed—that cost more than the average person made in a lifetime.

An image flashed upon Sheldon's mind, and he had to bite down the laughter. He could cut off some fingers from these gnarled, old socialites and they'd have new ones sewn on inside an hour. Hell, maybe they sold fingers at a Shoppers Drug Mart in a place like Whistler. This time the laughter refused to be denied and he barked out a short, boisterous bray. It was throaty, unfamiliar to his ears. Different enough to sap the humor from the moment.

He was quiet by the time he reached the pain relief section. He looked left and then right before twisting the cap open on a bottle of Tylenol Cannabis AM. With an eyetooth, he opened the foil seal. Using a perfectly fine thumb, he pulled the foil back to get at the synthetic cotton ball. A young woman started up his aisle toward him and stopped dead without speaking. She had on an employee smock, but her expression was not of indignation, no, she looked horrified. His appearance finally hit him: pale-faced, filthy with dried blood, boney scabs poking out from rough-cut nubs. Double the effect of the image in a classy place like Whistler.

He moaned. "I don't have any money and I have to help my family. Some bad people hurt me, and I can't go to the police," he said, the words tumbling out of him.

The young woman looked around behind her and then took the bottle from him after making certain nobody watched them. She pulled out the cotton and handed the bottle back to him before continuing down the aisle to a door marked EMPLOYEES ONLY.

Sheldon lifted the bottle to his lips and shook six pills

onto his tongue. The bottle went into his pocket. His tongue was so dry and sticky, the pills began to dissolve. He hurried to the drink cooler and grabbed a bottle of water—*only $12.99* according to the sticker. Uncapped, he began chugging, only now aware of just how thirsty he was. Half the bottle was empty before an ice cream headache struck him hard enough to make his vision swim and equilibrium teeter. His right arm reached and slammed nubs against a cooler door. A pained moan erupted up his throat.

He had to get the hell out of there, causing a scene would likely bring cops, which would keep him from doing this one selfless thing. He stumbled toward the section marked first-aid. There in the aisle, no longer worried about patrons or employees seeing him steal, he opened a bulk pack of gauze and began wrapping his wounds. He worked quickly, clumsily. The gauze had a chemical numbing agent that was active when damp and he nearly wept at the instant lessening of the continuous throb.

"What happened to you?" asked a man in a silky shirt and tight, tight slacks, fine loafers on his feet.

"Kristy Clarke," Sheldon said, and then added, "Can you rip me a few strands of tape?" He nodded down to the rolls of white tape beneath all the gauze and pain relief pads.

The guy was wide-eyed and did as he was asked. "I sold her a plot of land once," he said. "Sort of, she used the Dìzhǔ Corporation as a front, but it's all the same conglomerate."

Sheldon huffed. "I borrowed money to bet on a tip that I heard came right from her…now that I think about it, that's not a bad scheme. Fix horses and let slip bad information so that people borrow from you to take that very money to your bookies."

"Hold out your hand," the man said and got to within

an inch of touching Sheldon. "I'm not going to catch AIDS or Roman Fly Disease or something, right?"

Sheldon shook his head. "Outside this, and being overweight and selfish, I'm a model human specimen."

Within a minute, the man had both Sheldon's hands wrapped and taped. Sheldon dropped the empty water bottle as he started toward the exit, the pills in his pockets rattling like a maraca. As he was passing a till, another employee waved. This was a middle-aged man with the word MANAGER stitched on his chest.

"Hey! Stop! I'll call the cops!"

The man who'd helped to wrap Sheldon came forward. "I'll cover his stuff. He just about gave me the greatest anecdote for the..." The man wasn't done speaking, but Sheldon was out on the street and heard no more. He used his thumb on the keypad—until returned, his prints made him the keyholder—and opened the car door. The weed pills were starting to take effect and a tingly glow came upon his skin. When he was a kid, marijuana was illegal and looking at it now, he could hardly fathom that fact. It was a miracle drug that grew like crab grass. In one shape or another, it was in every pain medication on the market.

He poked the GPS to resume his journey. The car veered into the sparse traffic and continued northbound. He wasn't sure how exactly he'd find them, or how he'd outpace the meth head bikers—the Black Teeth—but he had to try.

Within twenty minutes of rolling just below the speed limit, the first clue came to him in the form of a cop car on the far side of the highway. It had its flashers on and was parked along a skinny gravel road a little way up. Two cops were in the ditch, shining a high-powered light onto something metal.

"Manual drive," Sheldon said.

The engine lulled at the sudden decrease in power

distribution. Sheldon stretched out and tapped the brakes, jerking the car—it had been several months since he'd driven anything. He all but stopped to rubberneck at what was in that ditch. It appeared to be a motorcycle. He rolled down his window and the scent of gasoline was heavy.

"Huh?" he said and continued onward, knowing now that he was closer than he could've hoped. Not far ahead, more lights shined, this time traffic was down to a lane. Flashlight beams danced around the ditch and nearby woods. He again stopped, a little less jerkily this time. His window went down the rest of the way and he leaned out, trying for a better view. It was hard to tell what he was seeing, and then he understood. A moving truck had been flipped. His heart again began beating in overdrive. "Come on," he mumbled, thinking he'd already missed his shot.

There was a single cop on the road waving people along. Sheldon dismissed her glowing baton and stopped. "Move it," she said.

"Just tell me nobody's hurt," Sheldon said.

"Nobody's there at all. Now, go!"

Sheldon put his foot on the accelerator pedal and moved forward. He began trying to map out what had happened. This triggered something he'd bet on with a few buds one night while hanging in the Monkey Lounge on the east end of Vancouver. A news update rolled by on the ticker that a government official had gone missing while surveying property just south of Pemberton. Tomoya Mori had pointed up to the screen and said, "Fifty bucks they find him mauled by a bear," and to this Sheldon responded, "Timeline?" Mori scrunched his face and then said, "Inside a week." Sheldon nodded. "All right, bet." They shook on it. All week they'd watched the updates and the oddity of the situation grow. The planned development of the land had to be halted and a perimeter fence erected thanks to extreme soil radiation. It was so bad they didn't have any idea on how to fix it. Sheldon owed Mori $30 as it was, and they'd bet on a hockey game for the final $20. It came out to a wash in the end.

What if Hannah and the kids had run into the forest? What if this was the spot the was irradiated? Jesus, would they come out looking like Lloyd Kaufman characters? It certainly was underdeveloped and under-treed, given how thick the forests were in government tree programs, was this the irradiated area?

Sheldon continued rolling, well below the speed limit, looking for a road and finding none. It had to be the one before the crash, near that overturned motorcycle, where that first cop had been. He turned around—performing a clumsy seven-point turn—and started back the way he'd come. The cops still had traffic down to a single lane and the wait was almost two minutes before he got onto the right side of where he needed to be.

Thankfully, the cop was gone from the road, as was the downed motorcycle from the ditch. Sheldon bumped carefully onto the single lane gravel path. The GPS monitor flashed red, suggesting that he was taking the car off-road. He ignored it and kept on, following his guts and its sense of hope, quickly coming to a fence with a cut chain and fresh tread marks in the ground.

"Bingo was his name-o," he said.

With his window down, he could hear a steady, rhythmic, hammering sound that was far from natural to the forest. He didn't want to give himself away, so he cut the nearly silent engine and quickly climbed out of the car and closed the door to douse the interior light and kill the ping-ping-ping. The Tylenol was in his system in a way that spoke full volume when he started to move around. Everything was fuzzy and heavy, but soft, it was as if his body had become soggy wool. Pleasantly soggy wool.

Sheldon stopped, panting as he leaned against the single remaining corner of a destroyed and dismantled home. He wondered, vaguely, if radiation caused a house to collapse and decided it didn't. He thought not. Hoped not. If he recalled correctly, it mostly worked at changing and destroying cells, but that might be a mis-memory. Over the years, he'd come to accept that his remembrances usually worked to suit whatever he was doing—scheming—at one time or another.

Sheldon curled around the corner to get a look up the hill. Three headlights from motorcycles shined on the front of a cabin. The rhythmic pounding sounds were the four bikers apparently trying to take down the front wall. He gasped. His family had to be in there…but the door was open. What in the hell were these maniacs doing?

It happened then, the doorframe and part of the wall burst inward on a booming crack. The bikers dropped their makeshift tools—all but one man who kept hold of an axe—and hopped onto the trio of motorcycles. The engines growled to life, and then one at a time, the Harleys roared up the hill and through the hole in the wall.

"Riding inside?" Sheldon said, confused.

He waited a few moments. The motorcycle sounds were entirely gone. Disappeared. Quiet reigned the lonely yard of the peculiar property. Sheldon pushed up from where he leaned and trailed after the bikers, and he assumed his family.

"Wouldn't they be shouting?" he whispered to himself as he closed in on the deck. "Screaming? They have to be in here?" Everything was in question.

He reached the deck and listened. Silence. Inside was dark but for a subtle green light rising from beneath the floor about halfway across the busy interior. Was radiation green? His mind began shouting that it was, but that voice was a voice that served only one person and never considered people he might endanger. He was done with that voice, for now anyhow.

He walked to the hole and down the steep ramp, following the light.

TEN

Skylar watched her brother and mother bury their faces in the crooks of their elbows, listening to the various unidentifiable rumbles of the forest, as well as the single all-too-definable rumble of the motorcycle engines. She closed her eyes as well, though did not lower her face, doing so would put pressure on that smarting rib and the pain was just now starting to slip into a simmering throb.

A wooden snap sang not far to her right, and she turned her head. Playing like a ghost amid the shadows was a deeper silhouette. It was massive, tall as a giraffe but thick as an elephant. Its long, long neck stretched high into the tree next to where they hid. Skylar was stunned silent. Its mouth opened, teeth and tongue and eyes glistening wetly in the moonlight as it snapped off a high, leafy branch. It chewed loudly enough that Gabe finally looked around.

"What the hell?" he said.

"Shh," Hannah said, and lifted her head—her legs were no longer dangling as she'd brought up her knees as if to get as compact as possible.

Skylar hit her shin and then pointed up to the giant beast. Hannah gasped and Gabe grabbed at her shirt, absently clinging to his mommy. The beast didn't seem interested in anything but its green meal, but that only made it a hair less frightening.

Back the way they'd come, the three motorcycles branched off in different directions, their engines roaring reports from varying angles. One set of lights blazed toward them where they hid, though the line was far from direct. The biker kept to the pond side of the trees and his shape was made entirely visible by the moonlight. His hair was shiny. His Harley likewise—polished rather than greasy. The black of his jacket seemed less black against the deepness of the rural night. He rolled slowly, head turning left and right in regular, monotonous motions.

Skylar thought of a movie a boy had once taken her to. She didn't recall the title, but the boy had insisted it was an Australian classic. It had featured violent bikers chasing down a mother and her small children. All along the way, the bikers raped and pillaged the sparse countryside while in pursuit. The film quality had been scratchy and fuzzy; the colors were muted, everything greyed out like pastels. The sound quality had been remastered, making the edges crisp, unbefitting of the images. Skylar closed her eyes, putting together what had to be dream math, her subconscious entwining two semi-related topics to present something new. Neon lights flashed on the backs of her eyelids, the double dose of trouble she was currently experiencing: DINO GRINDHOUSE.

Distantly, a shotgun blast rang out and echoed over the plane. If the nearby biker heard, he didn't react to it. The blistering tattoo of his engine growled and grumbled, growled and grumbled as the man at the handlebars squeezed and then coasted, squeezed and then coasted. He'd gotten to just about in line with the Lauries and the dinosaur when he stopped and stared into the rippling water of the pond—or perhaps lake? There was no way for Skylar to know for sure from the little bit she'd seen.

Next to the family in the tree, the huge animal ceased eating and grew almost silent. Its inhalations and exhalations were nearly inaudible above the motorcycle engine. Something in the pond moved, sending out cascading waves. The biker reached into a saddlebag and his hand came out holding a handgun of some fashion.

He aimed in the general direction of the movements in the water, his attention intent, pinpointed.

A tenth of a second after another, larger splash played out, the giant animal that had been grazing the high trees stomped forward three steps and then swung its great head at the biker. It missed but sent the man off his machine in surprise and a dust cloud into the air.

"Smoly crowly," Skylar said in wonder.

The biker backpedaled and swung around the arm holding the weapon. He began firing. The blasts were momentous in the quiet night. The muzzle flashes played halos in afterthought, as if burning holes into the film of the atmosphere. The giant animal got two thirds of the way through another swing before it reared back and spun on its heels, taking five great strides in retreat, into the forest. When it had come out into the moonlight, it revealed a rough and scaly body, meaning at least one of those shots had had to have been lucky and hit something tender.

The water began rippling out once more. This time a beast burst from its depths and charged at the biker. He squeezed anew as he scrambled in reverse, kicking at the heavy sand for purchase. The beast from the water looked a bit like a crocodile, though its snout was much longer and its body proportionately skinnier. Its legs motored, revolutions nearing full circles. It was out of the water and onto the beach in a blink. Its great jaws snapped onto the biker's kicking legs. He growled wordlessly, though somehow captured every nuance of the language of pain. The jaws opened a moment before snapping closed again with a better angle.

"Yo!" Gabe shouted and grabbed at Hannah as the large herbivore stomped back out of the tree line and made for the biker. Instead of swinging its head, it stamped with a calculated foot. It nailed in passing the tree and Hannah went flying off while Skylar and her brother managed to cling on.

Hannah screamed briefly and then moaned upon landing. All the action near the pool ceased for the moment—aside from the biker's lifeblood pouring free so quickly that the man had lost consciousness. The big foot of the huge beast then stamped down on the beast chomping at the biker. This snapped its jaws together, which in turn separated abdomen from hips. The crocodile-like creature snorted and growled, spinning to its right as it was driven deep into the sand. The big herbivore turned again, swinging its great tail before charging into the forest, directly toward the deformed tree with the handy basket.

"Look out!" Skylar whisper shouted.

Hannah had little time to avoid the falling foot, but did, though a jagged corner of the creature's clawed toe snagged on her shirt. She was lifted high and then thumped down once, twice, thrice, as the beast took long strides. On the fourth step, Hannah was flung deeper into the woods as the massive creature continued down its path.

"Mom?" Gabe said, that single word harboring a mix of terror and agony.

Skylar looked around before her gaze came back to Gabe. She was frantic, paralyzed beneath her neck by trembling soreness being aggravated by the tense situation. "What'll we do?"

"I don't know. I don't know," Gabe whined.

"Can you get her?" Skylar said, sobbing around the word.

"I don't know," Gabe said, lower, almost mouthing it.

Skylar said nothing to this and looked out into the darkness. Less than a minute later, a fresh scream filled the night.

ELEVEN

Hannah awoke on the forest floor, her body thrumming and her head swimming. The ground beneath her was stiff and yet damp, though not rocky or entirely firm. She'd bounced along mentally with the beast's foot for a single fall but then blacked out. Now, awake and feeling lucky to be alive, she took three deep breaths. Losing consciousness as she had made her think of those videos of musclebound men passing out on rollercoasters. Of course, rollercoasters were pretty much always safe, and her current predicament was far from safe.

And just how far was she from her kids?

Hannah rolled to her right in order to look back in the direction she'd come from, though she had no way to know for certain the animal hadn't turned, hadn't flung her sideways. Her eyes scanned the darkness, but she didn't get a chance to look high into the trees before a new subject stole her attention.

Not nearly far enough away for any kind of comfort was a brown creature with big black eyes that glinted the heavy moonlight pouring through the green canopy high above. It had a body like a worm, though was fortified with plates, and beneath were countless spindly legs. Two long antennae bobbed before its face. Its mandible was long and dripping. Fangs rose in jagged spikes from its underbite. Two arm-like protrusions stretched from its abdomen like postscript additions. Hannah moaned in a deep inhalation, and then bellowed a fantastic scream.

The insect shivered, jerking away its upper half before launching itself onto Hannah. The goop from its snapping jaw rolled over her face like molasses, burning her eyes and irritating her skin—whatever this thing normally ate, it had a weaker constitution than human flesh. She spat at the fluid passing between her lips. It was sticky and tasted like how sunbaked fish smelled: primordial, oceanic, gag-inducing. Its countless little feet scratched at her hands and chest. Her arms were stretched, elbows locked outward, keeping that angry mouth away from her face. She was succeeding, for now.

The insect screeched in her hands. Its backside slithered up onto the bare skin of her tummy, beneath her torn shirt. It was cold and rubbery, damp like everything else in this impossible place. Hannah belted free another scream.

A new scream came back at her. This one from high, high above. The insect froze in her grasp, its drool still playing down onto her face in a putrid cascade. Sensing the change, Hannah bent her elbows and attempted to fling the insect to her right. One of its weird little hands clamped onto her wrist as she rolled sideways. The hold was short-lived. The screamer from the sky swooped down, so big the cutting of air was audible, and snatched the insect. That little hand scratched into Hannah's wrist before it let go, gouging the soft flesh.

The fresh pain in her wrist had her hissing. The stinging in her eyes had her wiping her face. The soreness of her journey on the giant herbivore's foot was playing through her body in throbbing waves. The unreality of what was happening crashed in and on her, and she knew little beyond that she had to move, had to find shelter. In semi-blindness, she pushed to her feet and started running. She needed a tree. Once she was safe and had her bearings, she could locate her children and backtrack out of this place.

But which way were the kids?

Which way was the door?

She spotted a thick tree with gnarly, low-hanging

branches, and for a moment thought she'd stumbled upon the tree they'd climbed as a family. When she craned her neck, however, she saw neither Skylar nor Gabe, and the branches did not match, there was no fortuitous basket. Still, up was infinitely better than down. If nothing else, dating that dud was now coming in handy. She reached up and grabbed a scruffy limb—now that she'd touched it, she understood this was not even the same breed of tree as the other. She got to her knees after swinging her leg while pulling upward. Every movement sang fresh notes of pain. Steady, about four feet from the ground, she reached for the next branch.

This one was scruffy, like the last, but different. It almost felt like feathers beneath her hands, and it wasn't nearly as stiff. She pulled her weight. The branch began to move, rolling toward her. Hannah gasped and let go, stumbling and falling those hard-earned feet to the forest floor. Dropping next to her was the corpse of a strange looking bird. The impact sent huge, gooey maggots up to the surface of its flesh, as if rising for air; at first from a wound and then from the long beak. Its rotten eyeballs oozed out from their sockets as maggots squirmed and spilled free in a frenzy of fester.

Hannah rolled sideways again—the simplest way to put distance between herself and danger. Her elbow had joined the chorus of pain the moment she moved. She attempted to clear her mind, tried to understand well enough that she might survive this place. Gross as that corpse was, she had to get up a tree. She pushed herself upright and paused for a moment to gather her breath and slow the spin currently teetering her equilibrium.

Skittering motions and sticks snapping behind her got her moving. She took hold of that same low branch and pulled, no room for pain. She reached for the second branch after only a moment's inspection—it was too

dark to be certain she wouldn't grab another corpse—
and latched on and lifted as she kicked. At ten feet from
the ground, she decided that would do for now.

Leaned back, Hannah scanned the forest for signs of
life as she huffed and panted against the effort and hurt.
"Okay," she whispered. There had to be something she'd
learned that would help her now, some buried nugget
needing unearthing. But what was it? "Dammit."

Not far and coming her way, biggish footfalls
crackled through the forest.

Though agnostic and leaning toward atheist, she said,
"Please, god."

TWELVE

Skylar watched her brother as he climbed nimbly out of the tree after saying only, "You stay here." She was too scared to reply. Instead of speaking, she gently brought her knees up to her chest and pressed her back against the tree. He was visible again four or five steps after touching down. Long, strong legs carried him quickly, with the agility of an animal that belonged in a thick forest.

Skylar took a deep breath through her nose and mouthed, "Come on," without making more than a peep.

Within seconds, Gabe was to the downed motorcycle. Crouching, he reached his right hand blindly into one of the saddlebags, his head darting back and forth, the hatchet in his left hand. Seeing the fear in those motions made Skylar cringe. Gabe brought something small and glinting out of the bag, looked at it, and then flicked it open. A flame danced. He nodded and pocketed the lighter. He reached in again and then pulled out something cloth. Jerking his head, though less quickly now, Skylar wished he'd hurry the hell up. She'd never been so scared in her entire life. Gabe brought out a case on a strap and slung it over his neck.

"Okay, you got it, let's go," Skylar whispered, voice like a mouse fart during a church service.

Motorcycles growled in the distance. Something screeched high up in the sky. Then, unmistakably, Hannah's voice rang out with a shrill scream. That scream put Gabe into overdrive and a new set of shivers into Skylar's blood.

He grunted as he lifted the bike to flip it to get at the other saddlebag. He came out then with a handful of something. He ran to a nearby tree and used the hatchet to chop down a limb about as thick as a baseball bat grip. He ran back to the bike and dropped the hatchet—he needed both hands.

"What are you doing?" Skylar said.

He wrapped the piece of cloth around the end of the stick as he circled the Harley for a better angle and shoved the stick into the pierced tank. He then ran to the tree, the hatchet in the back of his pants.

Skylar watched him wide-eyed, mouth agape, looking for the right thing to say to make him get back into the tree. He looked up at her. With his free hand, he pulled out two extra clips to the handgun that lay somewhere nearby and the lighter. He then unslung the case from his shoulder.

"There's two clips down here in case we find the gun. There's a Zippo lighter. This case…I think it's binoculars. You want me to throw the stuff up to you? Will you catch it?" he said.

"Not the bullets," Skylar said, envisioning a spontaneous firing of every round.

Gabe palmed the case and tossed it up. It landed safely enough that Skylar only had to keep it from bouncing away. He then lit the cloth he'd wrapped around the stick, currently sitting on the sandy ground. The flame whooshed in a fantastic ball before settling.

"Here comes the lighter," he said.

It came into view and Skylar snatched at it, bobbling it, but not losing it. "Got it," she said. Speaking at even indoor volume made her ribs ache.

"Good. If I yell because I'm lost, or something else, you have to climb down and light the motorcycle on fire so I can find my way back. Okay?" he said.

"No, but—" Skylar said, but was cut off as Hannah screamed again.

Gabe took off with the torch. Skylar wanted to beg him back, but she also needed him to go save their mother. Now that he was gone, she felt so utterly alone she almost wished the bikers would come close enough that she might see their headlights, know that the fresh darkness that enveloped the forest anew was only temporary. Headlights were a human thing, made by people—well, machines, but people made the machines—and humanity was an affront to dinosaurs. The two pieces of animalia did not mix, did not mingle.

Though it was too dark for use, she opened the binocular case. "Oh," she said, and flicked the lighter. They weren't binoculars. They were night vision goggles and according to the small stamp on the top, they belonged to Vancouver PD. That was too much to think about at the moment. She found the power button in the firelight and turned on the goggles. A green glare shined from her lap. She closed the Zippo and stretched the rubber straps over her head. They fit loosely, so she tugged at the dangling rubber tails. The goggles cinched up and she saw deep into the night.

"Oh. Oh. Oh shit," she whispered.

When she was a kid, she'd gone camping with her father in one of the green spaces that had existed within the city limits. He'd said, "Let me show you a trick." She didn't argue. She was only little and back then, her mostly absent father was something like a hero—him alongside a handful of cartoon characters. They sat side-by-side in the doorway of the tent. He grabbed the big plastic flashlight he'd brought along and said, "Now, would you believe me if I said someone's watching us?" The wording had been freaky, but her father was smiling so she shook her head. He liked to kid, that was his way. He clicked on the flashlight and what seemed like a thousand little green eyes reflected in the dark.

There weren't as many things out there as there had been raccoons on that campsite, but there were significantly more than she was comfortable with. With cautious fingers, Skylar turned one of the rings on the lenses—she'd felt them while slipping the unit onto her head. Gabe hadn't been all wrong about them, they were indeed binoculars, of a sort.

Zoomed in, she watched a tight pack of four-foot dinosaurs. They popped and bounced along the forest floor like chickens in a barnyard. They had feathery bodies and sharp looking beaks beneath rubbery noses. They were circling a larger animal. From that angle, she could see only the head, which was about twice the height of the heads on the bird-like things' shoulders. Both sides snapped aggressively, though even from fifty yards away, it was obvious one side was in self-preservation mode. Skylar turned away when the feast really began, but her ears caught a keening, high-pitched cry of death.

She looked in the direction they'd come from, and she spotted one of the motorcycles. It was the one with an extra rider on back—assumedly his bike hadn't made it when her mother ran it off the road. The driver was rolling great circles while the one on the back aimed at the pond with a stubby stick she had to assume was a shotgun.

"You fight," she whispered, hoping the thing holding their attention was the same thing as before, now moved a good ways from where she currently sat.

A shot boomed—though the report was subdued by distance—flaring bright green into her eyes. Skylar squinted against it. A huge crocodile-like beast charged up onto the shore. The man with the stubby sawed-off shotgun began firing with something smaller and quicker. The beast took a few rounds before slowing. It made a noise between a honk and a growl. This made Skylar wonder if they hadn't stepped through a portal to another universe, as that sound seemed nothing like the rough and gravelly voices of the crocodiles she'd seen at the zoo.

The motorcycles stopped rolling and both men jumped off. The driver pulled a long machete from somewhere on his person and cocked it back next to his ear. The other reloaded the sawed-off and stomped toward the injured and sluggish beast. The men got to almost snapping distance before a great flash of light accompanied an echoing blast. The beast made another noise and the man with the machete charged, poised to chop. He did in a great winding arc and the beast jerked and snapped. More handgun fire pelted the thing. Motions ceased for five seconds before the man with the machete resumed his attack. The beast had to be dead after all that.

"Dammit," Skylar whispered.

The bikers stowed their weapons and each bent next to the beast. They came up holding forelegs and screaming non-words. The act was savage and only got more off-putting. They held the legs above them and turned their faces as if to a showerhead. It was carnal, animalistic, psychotic. It seemed like they thought they could fight off the universe if it came to that and come out victors of the void.

"What the hell?" Skylar whispered.

From behind her, her mother's voice came to her again. Skylar pushed to her knees and groped blindly at the tree. She felt for the edge of the natural basket holding her and the trunk. She hugged the tree, fingers tight in bark grooves. With a good grip, she leaned to her left to peer into the forest, attempting to see her mother or brother. It was hopeless. Too much thick foliage, so she shifted to the right side of the tree. She leaned as far as she dared and gazed out into a sea of limbs.

She straightened. Carefully, she turned and leaned back against the tree. She sat there a moment and then shivered. Her head jerked left and right, it felt as if someone or something was watching her. She saw nothing and nobody untoward, and still, the feeling was alive and instinctual. She pushed to her knees. Leaned over the limb where she sat, there was nothing but forest floor beneath her.

Again, she sat back. The feeling was still there. Slowly, she turned to face the sky. Directly above her was a bird, no bigger than a blue jay. She let out a harried sigh. The bird looked like any bird from her life, but scruffier, perhaps a little more robust.

"I thought you were something scary," she whispered, still looking up.

Down the tree, hopping as if ignoring gravity came a second bird. The pair studied her with beady eyes. Then, two more joined from a branch that swung out toward the water. Five more flew in and landed next to their brethren. All had eyes on Skylar. The safety she'd felt upon recognizing that the birds were small fleeted a little more with each additional set of eyes watching her. Two more bounced down from higher up. Four more flew in. It was as if they had telepathy or communicated at an octave beyond Skylar's hearing.

She pushed away from the trunk The pain had been subdued into a throbbing, mostly.

The bird collective popped closer.

Skylar's heart rate thrummed as she rose to her knees, moseying away another six inches.

The birds once again matched her.

She scanned the darkness around her knees and snatched up the lighter once she'd spotted it. When she returned her attention to the birds, they'd moved much closer. Were they curious or malevolent, or a mixture of the two, or something else altogether? For a moment she imagined that these birds saw all the tiny organisms feeding on her skin and these microscopic critters were like chocolate to them. They'd pick her clean of the organisms and then of her flesh as well.

Foregoing comfort, forgetting her rib altogether, Skylar pushed off the side of the branch onto her pelvis. The rib squealed once she lowered onto it and her hands let go of their grip. A pained yip left her mouth. The fluttering of birds was the only sound she heard over her own moaning.

She was on the ground, feeling more than down and out. The first flyby fluffed out her hair. The second, a wing grazed roughly at her arm. The third clawed at the back of her head.

Though she did not yet have her wind back, Skylar began crawling; one thing on her mind: fire. Birds landed momentarily, just long enough to peck or scratch at the hair on her head. She brought her face up every few seconds to be certain she kept true to her path. Crawling was an awful way to move with a busted rib, and her speed was about a quarter of what it might have been. No physical activity had ever hurt this much.

"Leave me alone!" she screamed.

This added to the pain and she nearly toppled, her elbow pinning protectively over the rib. Birds landed in twos and threes, slashing and nicking. The gasoline smell came at her. She'd learned all about combustible liquids and gases in science class. When she was little, some people still had to drive gasoline cars. The stink of them drew her attention and had demanded an explanation from her mother—her mother who couldn't afford a car at all, not that she'd had anywhere to put one.

One bird grabbed her right earlobe and attempted to fly away with it. Instinctive reaction sent her hand up and her body down.

"Agh!"

Sweat rose from everywhere in plump balls that shined beneath the moonlight. The birds converged en masse like she was a dish of seeds. Skylar dragged herself forward while attempting to get as small as possible and yet keep in motion. Finally, the gasoline smell was everywhere, making her feel woozy and a bit fluish at the back of her throat. Still covering herself, she reached into her pocket for the lighter. Blood oozed from dozens of little strikes. She glanced up to locate the motorcycle—right there. She flicked the lighter and had to close her eyes to the flare of brightness within the night vision goggles. Splashing sounds began and there was no doubt these birds drew other attention, despite that they attacked her in near silence. Any second something would rise from the surf and swallow her, the knowledge of this had her hands shaking.

Skylar tossed the burning lighter in the direction of the motorcycle, mentally scolding herself because what if it went out? It didn't. Almost instantly, the vapor caught, ballooning outward and scaring off the birds while melting the peach fuzz from her arms and singeing much of the hair along her scalp.

She reared away, covering her gaze with her elbow.

The liquid gasoline lit in a fantastic plume then.

The heat and brightness were far too much. Rolling away, Skylar put her hands on her head and pulled off the night vision goggles. Little explosions popped here and there from the motorcycle. The front tire caught fire, and a long wheeze shot a flame as if from a torch. Skylar saw little of the world beyond the firelight, but for the moment felt safe.

An encroaching motorcycle engine cut the moment short.

2022 – 25 YEARS AGO

Mata Kaur shook as her hand hovered over the mouse's left key. The cursor was dead center on the send button of her Mozilla Thunderbird email account. The address bar had nine recipients. Three were federal branches of government, two were provincial branches, and four were to media inboxes—the latter were one part attention, one part protection. Everyone had been lied to. Her reports had been doctored, leaving her signature on the line of something she knew to be untrue. People would get sick and they would die because of this report, and if she did not stop it, she was as bad as the moneygrubbing county councilors who'd sold the plot of land—on the basis of finally passing a litany of health and soil tests. The land passed none, and yet, the deal was going through. Infant deformities flashed through her mind like a carnival freakshow; that land was thick with radioactivity.

She was the only one who could stop it now. Just that morning Mata watched one of her underlings on Vancouver AM stand next to a reporter at the highly radioactive site—a site they couldn't safely scour without gear they did not have on hand—and claim a clean bill of health. On the other side of the reporter was a councilwoman named Karen Bergen. She had huge white teeth and blonde hair. Blue eyes so deep they seemed almost to send out swimming invites.

"This site will be home to more than one hundred families when construction is complete. There'll be a soccer field, a dog park, and a private pond," Bergen said.

Mata nearly gagged at the thought of children rooting up a field that would warp their cells, make them ill, and ultimately kill them young. She quickly penned a note and attached the reports she'd sworn that she'd handed over all copies of. Not a complete fabrication; a copy was a physical thing, and no scan was physical until printed. They jumped mental hurdles to lie about safety; she jumped mental hurdles to ignore laws concerning insider information. The reports were printed, several copies, and her hurdles had been toppled. The digital versions were also now attached to the email she was about to send.

The repercussions would be big and painful. She'd seen the way people had been gotten to by governments. Vancouver had a way of taxing individuals for what they'd come to own when they didn't play nice. The police would watch for her, her family, and their vehicles. Though it happened rarely, her computer and hard drive might be confiscated, and analysts might happen upon something ruinous—it didn't matter that they'd have to plant whatever illegal element they'd need to find.

"Doesn't change a thing," she said and let her finger stab at the button.

For twenty seconds, the email offered the opportunity to be called back. She pushed from her desk and stuffed her hands in her armpits. The little message disappeared. It was done. Perhaps she was done.

Three minutes later, someone from CityNews called her and asked to go on record. She didn't hesitate. "Yes," she said. "Record now if you like." He then sent her a Zoom link and she spilled all the beans, named all the names.

By the end of the day, she'd done six interviews and ignored dozens of local calls. She'd spoken to someone from the province's forestry department and then a federal agent of undefined agency. To her surprise, she was taken in by authorities much higher than those local and provincial parties who might attempt her ruination. A reporter also suggested that if the same things happened to her that had had happened to Gerard Bear—currently doing six more years in Kent Penitentiary for incriminating items found on a laptop he swore he'd never owned—that perhaps British Columbians as a whole ought to follow money trails before casting stones.

The reversal was swift. The project was abandoned, and the government fenced off the offensive area. Until they knew of the exact nature of the issue, they preferred to leave it alone—something was fishy with the old Racicot homeplace but stirring up contaminated areas tended to lead to spreading said contamination, so they'd left it be. All this good news had Mata feeling okay. Her guard lowered and one night while taking what she thought was a regular city cab, she was robbed and murdered. She was found the next morning missing all her fingers and toes alongside almost three pints of blood. Her mouth had been sewn shut.

The news reported what they saw and what the police told them. Speculation was beyond most comfort levels and Mata Kaur's memory faded at the next high-interest event, which in this case was the Met Gala and all the fancy things those important people spent hundreds of thousands of dollars to drape upon their lithe bodies. And still, those fences stayed in place around the property, and the province refused to act on cleaning it up, suggesting the potential downside was great enough to redefine the location as protected lands.

THIRTEEN

Sheldon had gone in and out of the portal several times, trying to make sense of what happened when he passed through. The time shifted in great intervals on his side versus the far side with growling animals and raging motorcycles. Mere seconds became hours, though the time on his phone ticked by the minutes as he did, not the worlds. In the end, he'd spent several hours on the property and was starting to feel a bit iffy, and it wasn't from the rising sun. He decided there had to be something to the radioactive point he'd come to recall about the lands over here—it had been big news for about a week when he was a teenager—and swallowed down his cowardice to travel through and stay over there. The plan had always been to go looking for his family, but if he was going to stay over there, it couldn't hurt to weigh the pros and cons.

"No more stalling," he whispered. "You're bringing them back."

Once in the dune on the far side, he slunk to the dipped opening and looked out into the darkness. He saw things, big things, but they'd disappear into the shadows fast enough that he had to question his mind. Still, from the moment he stepped through the first time, he knew this was not the same place, or if it was, it wasn't the same time. The second time through he saw something that looked a bit like a heron, but was taller, bulkier, and had a damned iguana in its bill. He'd lived his whole life less than 100 miles from here, and he'd never seen a lizard that big outside a museum or one of the countless movie sets that took over parts of the city every day of the year, pretending to be more exciting, usually American, locales.

This had him extra trepidatious. The exhaustion of extreme pain and goodly blood loss did not aid in his reluctance to power on out there either. Instead, he sat and began popping Tylenol pills one at a time, swallowing them with tinny tasting saliva. They'd hit quickly enough and smooth out his kinks, the only worry was that they'd slow him down to be a sitting duck.

Thirteen minutes after taking the first pill, he began to doze. A small gust of wind played into the dune, smelling of fire and gasoline. He didn't react, it didn't seem all that unusual at the moment, nothing seemed much of anything right then. At the eighteen-minute mark, all six pills had hit and were mingling in a way that had his body tingling. Distantly, he heard all kinds of noises, some of them human and feminine, the kind of noises he'd hoped to impede if not stop. He leaned back into the stiff sand of the dune and closed his eyes, grinning as he slipped into unconsciousness.

FOURTEEN

Through the dense brush, Gabe pushed onward, listening for his mother—and anything else that might be out there. The poncho he'd wrapped around the branch for a torch head was thick wool and proved to be more than able at holding a smoldering flame. He'd considered lighting the entire forest up but decided it wouldn't go. This was a wet place, a rainforest perhaps. British Columbia had plenty of rainforest, sure, but that was up north. At least not during his time—he was starting to guess that was a time portal in the basement of the cottage that went way, way back or way, way forward. That foggy doorway they'd traversed remained a mystery only because it was tough to swallow going back in time.

"Gabe?"

He cocked his head to his right.

"Gabe?"

"Mom?" He moved toward the sound of her voice. Unthinking of keeping quiet, he tromped over the fallen twigs and sticks, creating a soundtrack to his movements.

"Up here!" Hannah said, whisper yelling.

"Let's—" Gabe began and stopped.

There was a yip and a humanistic groan, both sounded very Skylar. Hannah instantly began climbing down. Gabe watched her, almost dancing to hurry back to his injured sister, and handed off the torch when his mother touched down. A free hand would let him wield the hatchet better. Without word, they took three running steps before stopping abruptly.

Far away, though too close for comfort, a thick-sounding tree snapped like a warning shot before an incredible, bird-like roar played over the forest. Another, slightly smaller sound followed it. More trees snapped. Growls played into the forest, cutting through the foliage and finding terrified ears; it was like being the next victim and hearing the *ki ki ki, ma ma ma* the moment before Jason Voorhees appeared.

"What was that?" Hannah said.

More tree snaps rang out. Moving toward them. These trees sounded smaller, though were loud enough to crack and snap. Hoggish grunting drew nearer, closing in. Hannah squeezed Gabe's bicep—strong for a teenager, though what good was a human arm in a dinosaur world? Gabe cocked back the hatchet, as if this thing barreling toward them was a cedar stove-length waiting to be cut into kindling.

Suddenly, it was there. The thing was at least as big as an elephant, though shaped more like a football. It had a stubby face with an oversized jaw. A long and boney tail swung out behind it, clipping trees and nearly taking Gabe's arm off, pinging against the steel of the hatchet and sending it flying out behind him. This beast had zero interest in Hannah and Gabe.

"We need to get back in the tree," Hannah whispered and pulled Gabe.

Along the way, he kicked the hatchet in the dark, feeling the blade against the side of his shoe. He bent to grab it, stalling momentarily to find the handle.

"Come on!" Hannah shouted.

Trees snapped in a great cacophony behind them. Hannah yanked Gabe.

"I'm getting the—"

She yanked him again. The hatchet was firmly in his grip, though he flailed at his mother's motion. Hannah reached for the limb she'd only just climbed down from. Gabe followed. Tree branches continued to snap behind them, though they sounded smaller and of lighter constitution.

Great heaving breaths suddenly filled the forest. Hannah was onto the second branch and Gabe was crouched on the first when the huge, hideous face appeared. The beast's head was long, almost equine, but a row of hundreds of teeth played above a leathery upper lip. It had beady little eyes, and a row of feathers rimmed its otherwise bald scalp like a crown. It went three huge strides past Gabe and his mother—head to tail it had to be close to thirty feet—and stopped. It straightened its back and lifted its great head, its tail digging into the forest floor behind it. Its head was suddenly close to twenty feet in the air. It looked at Hannah.

Being up in a tree now seemed capital D dumb.

It lowered its face once more and spun a surprisingly lean circle amid the tightly knit trees. At that size, it had no business moving so quietly, or with such grace. It sniffed twice before exhaling through its nose. The flame of the torch danced, almost dying. Tentatively, as if testing, the beast reached out its tongue to touch the flame before sucking it back and jerking its face away. It turned its head sideways.

"Throw it!" Gabe said from below, looking up from around back of the branch, not seeing everything, but seeing enough to think he understood.

When he was small, a kid in an apartment half a block away used to take this mangy dog to the park. It was old and slow, until someone threw something. Then, as if it had been saving its energy, the old dog burst. Its grey legs moved like the stills of a penny viewer until it caught up with whatever was thrown. It didn't catch and it didn't fetch, instead the dog destroyed its prey. One time, three little boys were rolling down a hill and that dog decided they'd been thrown. It attacked. One of the boys had to have surgery to reconstruct his lips. Another needed thirteen stitches in his scalp. The third only needed new pants. The dog was detained and then killed.

This giant beast was no dog, but maybe…

"Throw the fucking torch, Mom!" Gabe shouted, squeezing his body against the tree's trunk.

Hannah cocked and threw the torch, losing her balance in the process and pitching her body in reverse off the branch where she stood. The beast turned again, disturbing not so much as a twig in the trees above it. It did not chase. It looked back and began sniffing for Hannah. Its face lowered.

Gabe had already hopped down. He pulled his mother until he knew she was following. They crawled over the sandy floor until they reached a large tree. Above them, the canopy of branches opened, letting the moonlight in. About ten yards away, slunk low against a tree was a lizard of some fashion, its tail coiled tight around its legs. Its face was all but hidden behind its legs. The pose was strangely akin to a housecat, though this creature was not sleeping. Gabe gasped quietly then as his gaze played further. There had to be ten of those things, coiled and hiding.

"We have to keep moving," Gabe whispered.

The beast behind them continued to sniff at the tree. Hannah crawled blindly, almost sideways, keeping her eyes on it. Once they got to about fifteen feet away, Gabe risked pushing upright against a tree. He pulled Hannah up next to him.

"We need to run. Quietly," he said, mouth tight to the side of his mother's head.

"I think that's a tyrannosaurus, or an Albertasaurus. When I was little, your grandparents took me to Drum…" she trailed, shaking her head. "You went there, too. I think?"

Gabe looked back at the huge beast again. He'd done virtual tours of many museums through school over the years. One was the Royal Tyrrell Museum in

Drumheller, Alberta. The museum was in Drumheller because the town was like dino central. So, yes, he had been there in a sense, and that beast before them very well could be a tyrannosaur or an Albertasaur, but what did that matter?

"Focus. We need to run," Gabe said again, shaking his mother while squeezing her bicep enough to steal her attention.

They did not run, but they did move quickly, and in near silence.

FIFTEEN

That motorcycle sound moved at locomotive speed, or seemed to; in her current state, she knew she couldn't wholly trust herself in relation to the world around her. And yet, she couldn't stem the rising tide of panic welling within her chest.

Looking to her left, right, behind her, Skylar didn't know where to go. The fire kept the birds away—and who knew what else—but would draw the remaining bikers toward her. She had to do something or this was it, this would be her end.

The tender and yet firm press of Abby's lips came to mind and Skylar knew then that she'd never feel them or any other lips again. This caused a physical ache that thrummed through her senses, almost as painfully as the injuries from the crash. She began hyperventilating, digging her hands absently into the sand.

Not far away, the motorcycle headlights played over a sand dune and trailed onto the lifeless water and surrounding beach. Something glinted. Something black. Her one chance.

She pushed to her knees and broke away from the comforting heat and glow of the fire. She picked up the tossed handgun. It was sticky with a mystery liquid she did not care to solve. She turned toward the onrushing motorcycle, aimed—generally—and squeezed. A round exploded out with more force than she had anticipated, but not enough to make her lose hold. The motorcycle kept coming, so she squeezed again.

Click.

She tried again.

Click.

She gave a single frustrated stamp of her foot—the

motion shooting pain into her chest and abdomen—before spinning and laboring back toward the tree. With the fire behind her, she saw the way without trouble, and then some. There was a dragonfly about the size of a kite perched on a downed tree limb that made her gasp. Its glassy eyes followed her. Beyond it, near the tree, was another set of eyes. They were small, though no less ominous. What animal they belonged to was beyond her sight. She rushed as best she could by three birds. None looked her way, as if hypnotized by the dancing flames. She reached the tree that had been their initial refuge.

Shadows enveloped everything and she stood aside to let the light play onto the prizes Gabe had left her. There were the clips, waiting to be loaded and fired. She changed the grip on the handgun and began yanking at the base. She'd seen enough movies to know the just of things, but they didn't really go over clip release—this was the first handgun she'd ever even seen in real life not holstered to a cop's hip. When the clip refused to budge, she took to prodding for buttons. She recalled people pulling back the top part—whatever the hell it was called—and tried that. The barrel slid before firing forward on a stiff spring, back into place.

The motorcycles were no more than twenty feet from where she stood. She fingered every nook and cranny and screw hole and rivet until her thumb found the button. It didn't press easily, was in fact so stiff she'd almost given up after three quick attempts, thinking it another rivet. The clip dropped into the sand at her feet. She stared dumbly a moment.

The Harley engines roared. She grabbed a fresh clip and tried to push it one way, then the other, and finally back around. It made her think of science class and dissecting and using old computers, the way the damned USB was never quite the correct way. She spun, aiming in only a vague sense. She squeezed the trigger once.

Click.

The bikers were so close she could see some of their features. Their faces glinted wetly between the firelight and the moonlight. They looked almost black, but that wasn't quite right and when she connected two dots, she understood. They'd bathed in blood.

"Jesus," she whispered and yanked on the barrel slider, working on the memory of countless movies celebrating America's favorite pastime: gunplay.

She aimed in the general direction of her targets. The biker—hadn't there been more?—had slowed to look at the bits of man and his burning bike. It wouldn't pay to lose one of her targets, or had she been seeing echoes? She couldn't trust anything, but she had to try to trust the heavy metal in her hands. Skylar squeezed the trigger three times. The gun jumped her arm several inches with each round. None hit the bikers. She finally saw them both again, and the one riding on the back aimed his sawed-off shotgun at her. She dropped behind the tree. Within a second, sawdust rained down upon her and the ripping echo of the shot slashed through leaves and into the forest.

"Stupid," she said beneath her breath as she crawled—this angle stung the worst of all. In hindsight, hiding seemed like the option she should've gone with. Then again, what was out there with her? She pictured her bed and closed her eyes as she slipped beneath an uprisen root, trying not to think about the little things she'd seen at the bases of trees in the city's many green spaces. She did not dare look around her, there was no way a bug hadn't called this space a home before she'd ever gotten there.

It was cool down there, damper, and there was a scent. She brought her gun hand up and looked to the space above her. Anything below her had to be small and had to be ignored…she simply needed it to be small and ignorable. If she managed to survive, she'd have nightmares until the end of time as it was.

Crunchy footfalls approached and Skylar watched to her right, waiting, waiting, waiting for a bike. One did not come. Instead, a bird popped around the corner. It was much bigger than the ones that had attacked her. She swallowed a dry lump.

It drew a step closer. Skylar took aim as light and engine sounds began playing into the blackness surrounding her. The bird abruptly turned, and the motorcycle burst out from around a few trees. The bird took flight. The driver lifted his arms to cover his face when those clawed talon feet rushed by. The Harley teetered. The man on the back took a shot with a handgun. The bird kept flying, though did so at no more than eight feet from the ground.

Skylar had no choice. She took aim anew and fired three rounds with her forearm steadied on the ground. Her hand went numb after that and her index finger refused to cooperate, despite that she totally damned well needed it to do so. One of the bikers was on the ground holding his leg and making a noise like a mechanized hog. The other stomped toward Skylar. She screamed and attempted to drag herself free of the space beneath the root. The biker saw this, and instead of firing, grabbed hold of her arm, yanking her upward.

Skylar wailed against the instant pain.

There was an audible pop when she came fully free. Up her legs and torso, footlong creatures—like a mix between a salamander and a spider, but with heavy armor plating—scurried, attacking her first and then the man. Skylar screamed again while the man let go to begin a jerky dance as he attempted to fend off the hideous things. That scent she'd smelled when climbing into the hole was tenfold now.

Little mandibles nipped and spindly feet scratched at

her flesh. She bounced and rolled, trying to free herself, no pain matched the disgusted terror of having those things on her. From above came an incredible series of squawks. Leaves and twigs rained down over them.

The shot man had crawled to his friend and was assisting with bug removal, he did not notice the mass of birds converging on them. The birds dived, landing and driving their beaks into the riding leather, then the flesh of the men. Skylar saw this, knew it was about to happen to her, and got to her feet. The huge insects were doing little more than sliding about her skin and inadvertently scratching her with their stiff-limbed movements; perhaps they were sucking those very same microorganisms she'd considered not ten minutes earlier. She broke around the tree, handgun still in her limp grip, and made for the fire.

A bird nailed the back of her legs as she ran. It sent her sprawling and rolling into the dry sand. She felt those spindly feet clinging to her like June bugs to a screen door. From the forest came growls and gunshots. Skylar was back to her feet in seconds. A bird snatched an insect from her hip, and the resulting scratch hardly sent her stride askew. She needed that fire.

Blood and sweat ran into her eyes and she swiped at her forehead with a dirty forearm. She stumbled and dropped. The heat of the fire was good and holy and cleansing, more than she could've hoped for. The birds left her alone and the bugs—more hideous in the firelight—began to depart her body. They burrowed into the sand. Suddenly she was free of anything untoward and alone.

Sitting where she was did not seem like a long-term solution. She again rose to her feet, this time snatching up the softened and hot to the touch night vision goggles. That heat had her wincing and shaking, and still she held tight. She broke straight ahead, into unexplored space.

The breeze of her run played against the goggles, cooling them enough to slip them onto her head and over her face. She found a low-hanging tree branch and reached up. The gasps and moans were audible but unavoidable as she climbed. Another branch drifted up at an intense angle. Skylar kicked and shimmied, the handgun tucked beneath her shirt. Her ribs had gone mostly numb when she wasn't reaching. They throbbed steadily when she stilled, but it was a trouble she could live with. Living was the goal, bring on more pain if the universe must— just not yet.

Not long after the gunshots ceased, the motorcycles revved to life—distantly, she thought she heard a siren of some fashion and she imagined emergency crews finding them. Pure wishful thinking, that. The motorcycle passed Skylar's hiding spot, causing her to close her eyes to its light. There had been no rider on the back. He'd be walking, looking for her. Over and over, a voice in her head said, "You have to kill him. Gabe and Mom will come to the fire. You have to kill him."

Did she really have it in her. Her night vision was an upper hand; she could angle a way that put her in little harm, but could she kill someone?

She sighed, wishing for fortuitous dinosaur attacks.

SIXTEEN

Hannah pulled Gabe to a stop as she stumbled against a tree. She was gasping, her head light and swimmy; this running could not continue. She'd never considered herself out of shape, but didn't test it, and now, stacking her abilities next to a fit teenager, she was feeling the hard punch of time and physical laziness.

Incredibly, Gabe seemed entirely unfazed by the effort.

Her throat felt burnt and rubbed raw. Her lungs felt frozen in place, as if they'd pinched tight as an Arctic blast solidified them. Saliva oozed from her lips; she spat, a string running from her face to the ground before breaking off. All around them little snaps promised creatures moving in the darkness.

"Mom. Mom, we have to move," Gabe said.

"Where?" Hannah said through a gasp.

The snaps and cracks and wheezy animalistic noises where impossible to ignore, and seemingly drawing closer.

"Look." Gabe turned Hannah's head with the nudge of his hand.

Through the dense foliage was a flickering light. Hannah swallowed against her sweaty mouth. She felt a bit like she was drunk, or more precisely, like that moment before vomiting after drinking too much.

"Sky lit the motorcycle. We have to run."

Hannah shook her head. "I can't run."

Gabe pulled her by the arm. "Mom! They're getting closer. Can't you hear them?"

Hannah wheezed a long, moist whine.

Gabe huffed. "Okay. Get to the light as fast as you can. Got it?" He lowered his face to look into his mother's eyes. "Got it?"

Hannah nodded.

Gabe reached into his pocket for his cellphone. He opened an app called COPS IS COMIN. He bounced ten feet in the opposite direction from the fire and tapped his touchscreen before breaking into a run with his phone held high above him in one hand. Cocked and ready, he held the hatchet with the other. Red, white, and blue light flashed while a siren rang through the quiet forest.

Hannah watched him for less than five seconds before she stumbled onward. Her brain screamed that she couldn't let Gabe do what he was doing. A matching voice screamed that she had to find Skylar.

With every sluggish step, her breath came back a little more, her lungs opened, and her mind cleared in equal measure. The fire ahead was not far, but neither was the growl of a motorcycle, though it sounded as if it was peeling after Gabe. At less than fifty feet away, she could smell the gasoline and the smoke. The flames were clearly visible, the chemical hues of green, blue, and yellow dancing within the reds and oranges. Not the kind of fire to roast weenies by.

Distantly, behind her somewhere, Gabe kept up running—she had to hope—while the app sang out the imitation emergency siren. On and on she pushed her drained body. She wanted to call out for Skylar but swallowed the urge. She needed to get away from the beasts in her wake—man and otherwise—she had to make what Gabe was doing work with her silence.

"Call in thirty steps," she whispered and began counting her footfalls silently. She inhaled deeply after thirty steps and got out only, "Sky—!" before an arm encircled her shoulders.

"Hush," said a deep, grunting, manly voice, lips wet and gooey against her ear. "Do as I say." He brought the sharp double barrels of his shotgun against her chin.

"This close, your head'll be mist if I squeeze this trigger. Understand?"

Hannah, panting, said, "Yes."

"Walk."

They moved. Hannah felt various body parts touching her. The rough zippers of his jacket grated against her flesh. He smelled like melted plastic and rubbing alcohol. His breath was a bouquet of burning garbage that made her think of an information session she'd visited back before Skylar was born. Smoked drugs always smelled like something else, dependent on which chemicals were used in the manufacturing process.

They stepped into a clearing, the burning motorcycle only ten feet from them, shining brightly and crackling. The tires were the biggest source of flames. They'd burned down to about half what they had been and would go on burning a little while longer by the looks of things.

"Call out the bitch," the biker said.

"No," Hannah said.

"We came for money, not blood. Call her out."

"She doesn't have money?" Hannah said.

The sawed-off shotgun pressed tighter to her flesh. "She's got Chedder's gun. We take care of that, then we worry about two hundred K."

No doubt now, it was the check. Sheldon's apologetic face rose upon the wall of her mindscape like a drive-in movie. He'd worn it so, so often way back when. Hannah had come to hate it more than all his other expressions. That phony regret. Those moments after understanding he'd hurt them and faced anger, faced punishment for his actions. Never had it been regret; he was incapable of true regret.

"Call her." The barrels nodded her head upward. "Now."

Hannah closed her eyes. What choice did she have?

Death or endanger her daughter.
"Fuck you," she said.
The blast was incredible.

SEVENTEEN

Gabe never questioned whether or not he could outrun the creatures of the forest. He, like so many athletic young men, assumed nothing could possibly catch him. His lungs felt good and his legs were pumping on a modulated adrenaline flow. He'd run track every year until his senior year when some of the practices conflicted with lacrosse and his track coach gave him an ultimatum—certainly assuming he knew which was more important to Gabe. Gabe could be an elite runner, or just another member of a team sport nobody really cared about.

"Don't see how people caring about runners once every four years makes it as popular as you think," Gabe said before he left the field and a stunned coach behind.

Thankfully, now, his desertion of the track had only been nine months earlier. Double that thankfulness that his lacrosse coach had them run five miles a day, five days a week. Gabe guessed he could probably run twenty at a fairly high level of speed, though had never attempted it.

A downed tree offered a dozen glinting eyes, small ones, creatures dwelling in the deepest shadows to be safe from larger predators. Gabe leapt over the tree easily.

The app on the phone kept him from hearing much, but he sensed he had a tail on him. He glanced over his shoulder. In the moonlight, nine more sets of eyes glistened from shadowy faces standing about 5 feet off the ground. These eyes were much, much larger and scarier than those that had been under the downed tree. Gabe pushed harder. He glanced back again after a dozen steps at full throttle. The pack had gained on him.

Seeing this made him stumble.

"Shit," he hissed and closed his eyes to push. When he opened them and looked back, he had to lunge sideways, away from a swinging arm with three fingers and long, curving claws. Like dragon talons, *they have dragon talons!*

He had to get high and hope these things couldn't climb. He continued running, feeling their near misses, hearing their snapping jaws and grunting breaths. They didn't sound like they were tiring. Not that he was either. And still, if he kept this up, they'd get bored of the chase and drag him down because it was all too clear they had another gear.

A suitable tree came into view. It was stubby and angled like a steep ramp. With the correct tilt, he'd be able to run halfway up the tree before he'd even have to use his hands. Though, they'd have the same circumstances, and what if they were much faster on their fours than he was?

Imperfect, but this tree was all he had.

A step before he reached the base of the tree trunk, he swung the hatchet out behind him in a sideways rainbow arc, clipping two of the beasts, missing the lead one completely. It snapped a great set of carnivore fangs at his arm, slicing an intense groove into the meat just above his elbow. He screamed and nearly dropped his phone, though managed to keep hold while losing the hatchet.

The phone went between his teeth the moment he had to bend over to grab where the tree had gone on to attempt righting its upward course, to chase after sustenance from the sun. Moving like a monkey, he looked behind him. The beasts were right there, single file like a class trip mounting a school bus. They were only as fast as Gabe; this despite that he'd gone down to about a quarter of the pace he had been moving. The trunk beneath him turned starkly upward, and Gabe leapt to grab for a branch that crossed over the crooked tree beneath him.

He caught the limb after slamming his forearms and then did a pull-up and then some on top of that, swinging his body to wrap his legs and hook his ankles together. He saw the new light then. A biker was rolling his motorcycle closer, engine dead, light cutting into the deep woods like a spinning blade through lunchmeat. The beasts began jumping and falling from the crooked tree, trying to reach the branch Gabe was currently shimmying along, upside down. Several times now he nearly dropped his phone, twice he'd bitten into the poly-glass screen, feeling the telltale cracks through his gums.

The biker dismounted but left the light burning. He stepped sideways to get a clear line at Gabe. Gabe watched his hands come up in that unmistakable way that screams 'I'm gonna shoot you!'

Flitting across his subconscious was the torch his mother had thrown. It hadn't helped much then, beyond letting his mother's fall from her branch prove fortuitous, but these were different beasts and they'd been hot for something making that godawful racket.

The biker banged off three rounds. Two missed completely and the third struck the branch next to Gabe's right hand. He clutched with his left and took the phone from his mouth. The beasts continued leaping beneath him, with each miss, they started over. Another shot hit the branch near his face, this time raining wood chips onto him in a short-lived soft, moist hailstorm. He leaned back and lobbed the phone underhand at the biker some twenty-five feet below. It was still flashing and sounding off when it landed at the biker's feet.

The beasts quit jumping and looked at the phone less than a second before switching their focus and converging on the biker. He got off eight rounds, which deterred but two of the beasts—they'd taken multiple shots each and were good for little more than a carnivore's supper now.

Gabe didn't let himself watch for long. He shimmied across the branch to the tree next-door. He climbed down as quietly as he could, free falling the final twelve feet—onto his butt, mostly—for lack of another option. He popped up and began sprinting. He didn't dare look, knowing those things had switched focus, knowing those things were going to chase him down and devour him— they'd played enough, surely.

The alarm had quit its squeal about two minutes after being tossed and Gabe dared a glance over his shoulder. He saw nothing and heard nary a footfall nor a gunshot. They weren't chasing that he could tell. He faced forward just in time to see the tree he was about to nail with an unprotected face. His shoulder bounced off as he veered to his left and he landed with a thud as his feet twisted up. Unable to help himself, he gasped loudly where he lay on the forest floor. Great honking intakes of air refused to fill his lungs. His legs went to jelly. If they were coming, they'd come now.

No beasts approached. He heard nothing. He saw nothing. Once all was right in his chest, Gabe pushed to his knees as his body finally began to cooperate with him. He inhaled deeply through his nose and smelled a dirty fire. Up to his feet, he sought firelight and found it through the thick forest. Gabe began to run once more.

EIGHTEEN

Sheldon blinked awake feeling all right. His missing fingers throbbed a ghostly tune but the cannabis extracts in his system had that tune coming through a distortion filter. Not pain or even irritation, what he felt was a giggly vibration. He'd had more than he should have for a rescue mission, but he'd had just enough to let him move his body.

He looked around the sand dune. Still dark. He hadn't slept long. He rolled sideways and put his right hand down to steady himself. That ghostly tune changed and the sudden jolt of pain awoke him some. He'd come to this place for a reason and that pain was a reminder of what would happen if the Black Teeth got ahold of his family. Once up to his feet, he had to lean with the bases of his palms against his knees. A wet and hot deluge of vomit barreled up his throat; so bountiful, it shot from both his nose and mouth. It tasted like ketchup and meat flavoring. A ball of partially digested cheese oozed from his nostril until he gave what his father had called a 'farmer blow.' He stumbled out between the dune drifts, tripping over a piece of rope driven into the sand and nearly falling.

Blinking wet, wet eyes, he bent to look at the rope. A little tug brought Dr. Pierre Racicot's painted turtle to the surface. A tiny thing…but wasn't this a place of massive beasts? He'd seen them before he reloaded on the good Tylenol, hadn't he? His mind was scattering bits and pieces in a way he couldn't quite put together.

Sheldon dropped the turtle and scanned the darkness, there wasn't much doing, and that in itself was a touch unnerving. His entire life he'd been able to see bright lights in one direction or another. Now all he saw was the moon, trees, and a longish body of water. On the surface of that water, ripples played slowly, carrying an orange hue that did not belong to the moon.

More blinking, he swiped at his eyes, running the rough and filthy bandages over his flesh. That flicker looked a bit like firelight, but what was causing the water to move?

"You don't want to know, Shelly," he said.

At a distance impossible to gauge, a motorcycle engine rumbled. As much as he dreaded seeing the Black Teeth again, it's what he came to do. No more cowardice, no more selfishness, he had to fix this situation or die trying. He meandered away from the water some and then started toward the dense tree line. The scent of burning came to him: rubbery with whiffs of gasoline. This was the right direction.

Sheldon paused a moment outside the forest to bring to mind Gabe and Skylar, as they'd been as babies and toddlers, before Hannah did the smart thing. He'd been furious with her. He'd promised to take custody. He'd sworn up and down that he was going to make her pay. He'd done all of this in his mind in the span of about twelve seconds before he realized she was doing him and his preferred lifestyle a favor. He had the gift of gab and women all over were susceptible to smooth talking, moderate good looks, and a great grin.

He put that grin on his face now, or tried to. It had been soured by painful reality and the passing of time. Grimacing, sluggish, and with nobody to sweettalk, Sheldon stepped into the shadows of this strange place.

"You will do right even if it's the last thing you'll do," he whispered, psyching himself up.

2027 – 20 YEARS AGO

The loud Harley motorcycle rolled up. The man behind the handlebars held an envelope out before him as he pulled to a stop. The two young men standing in wait were first generation Canadians, born of Vietnamese parents. Their mother had died and their father—who'd been their mother's senior by thirty-one years—was coping, poorly, with delusional disorder. The boys had dropped out of high school to work at the docks at fourteen and fifteen—some five years prior. They were poor, dumb, and desperate, so when they showed up at Vô Vọng—a bar around the corner from the bachelor apartment they shared with their father—and a white man wearing all black leather approached them about a quick job to make fast bucks, they had little choice but to accept.

That had been three weeks prior. Now a Harley and a GM truck were meeting them in a pissy scented alleyway with their payment for deeds done. The motorcycle rolled away, the biker keeping his expression cold and focused. The driver of the truck handed over the envelope with a big, nasty grin on his face.

"Be smart, now, boys," he said before hitting the gas and exiting the alleyway.

The elder of the brothers opened the envelope to reveal a wad of paper cut to dollar bill size. They processed what had happened silently for no more than twenty seconds before bright lights filled either end of the alleyway.

"Bob and Peter Ngo, put your hands up, you're under arrest for murder!" The voice saying this had boomed and shook the brothers deep into their cores. Though the brothers still weren't quite getting it. From either side, two men approached—one wearing black motorcycle leathers. Peter being a modicum smarter than his brother understood it then.

They'd been paid to dump a pair of bodies and were being framed for the murders by the man who'd hired them to dump the bodies—though he still didn't clue in that the man in leathers was a cop himself.

"Put that gun down!" the approaching cops shouted in unison.

Bob dropped the envelope. Peter had nothing to drop.

"Don't make us shoot!" one of the cops said.

Peter and Bob put their arms high.

"I said drop it!" the other cop said.

A steady whine played up Bob's throat.

The shots rang out, each cop picking a brother and filling his abdomen with rounds. The brothers dropped in the dim alleyway—Bob spinning and jerking his head around. They were dead before they touched the filthy concrete. The two cops that had stood back approached with handguns that would match the murder weapon that had killed two Royal Canadian Mounted Police detectives who'd been on a drug buying sting. Not one of the four cops ever expected that Bob Ngo was so desperate to be rich, he'd done something even dumber than dump two dead bodies on a delayed payment scheme.

In his headband, he wore a small camera, streaming to Twitch in hopes of gaining an audience, then fame, then all the money that went with fame. The four police were recorded murdering the Ngo brothers. One had even been recorded at the initial meeting and then at the warehouse where the bodies had been kept.

One of six viewers of the Twitch stream collected the data and presented it to the CTV News group, fearing that the police would get rid of him as they had the brothers. The news aired and for three days public outcry demanded the heads of the four officers involved in the murders of the brothers—and almost certainly the detectives. The Vancouver Police began an investigation that ended in four resignations. No charges were brought up. Nobody seemed to notice because Jessica Thibodaux's—an actor in an upcoming Marvel flick— sex tape had leaked and took over the headlines for most of a week.

Out of work and out of reach of the evidence locker and its mountains of illegal drugs, the four former cops were left unmoored and uncertain, wearing the leathers full-time now with no reason to switch into uniforms.

Kristy Clarke approached them two months after the smoke dissipated, offering them a sort of retainer. They would be her men when she couldn't trust anyone else. They would also become almost untouchable again. Hiding behind wealth was the second best place to hide a criminal—the first, of course, being behind a badge. They lived in one of Kristy's buildings and had run of the subbasement of another of her buildings. Whenever called upon, they did as asked. Between those times, they burned out their brains and rotted away their teeth sucking on glass pipes.

NINETEEN

About a million scenes from movies and TV ran through Skylar's mind. The biker holding her mother had walked right by her and now had his back to her, unnoticing and vulnerable. Still, the man had a sawed-off shotgun pointed to Hannah's head. Skylar's first impulse had been to step forward and lay down the weapon, but unlike Hollywood clips, the bad guys did not always have to lose. The good guys didn't even need to put up a fight. Not in reality.

She steadied herself. The forest floor was busy with twigs and leaves that might give her away. She mapped her first two steps and took them trying to fix her mind on an idea: one life was worth taking if it saved two, especially in this circumstance.

"Call out to the bitch," the biker said.

"No," Hannah said.

Skylar gritted her teeth and mapped two more steps. Her foot came down onto the sandy floor, crunching at a hidden twig that seemed like a bullhorn squawk right then, but at the same moment, the biker leaned his face against Hannah's cheek and said, "We came for money, not blood. Call her out."

"She doesn't have money?" Hannah said.

This paused Skylar. Perhaps there was still hope here. If her mother gave this psycho and his friends access to her bank account, then maybe they'd let her go.

Could it be so simple?

A taunting voice in her head began cackling madly at this. She looked at the ground and picked two more footfalls, wishing for silence. The universe obliged.

"She's got Chedder's gun. We take care of that, then we worry about two hundred K." The biker was moving as he spoke, and the way Hannah's head lifted suggested he'd pressed the barrels to her chin.

At that moment, her subconscious was so indescribably mad at her father, it seemed her head might burst—just as her mother's might. All this was happening because of her father. The anger made her hasty and she took three quick steps—quiet, but not silent.

The biker obviously didn't hear and said, "Call her."

The barrels nodded Hannah's head upward again.

"Now," the biker said. His voice was strange. So wet. So unhuman.

Hannah pushed against the biker and said, "Fuck you."

The biker had his attention on her solely and Skylar did what she had to. Both hands on the gun, she brought it up—in an instant, her mind jumped all the necessary hoops—and squeezed the trigger. The biker launched forward into the sand—no Hollywood dying here—landing heavily and motionlessly. Something flipped in Skylar, and she screamed, charging toward the corpse. Still using both hands, doing so by necessity in fact, she put six rounds into his back. The flesh jumped and a little spout of blood popped up from the first, rising about a foot before falling and pattering onto the leather of his jacket. The others entered the man with no pressure in the pipes.

"Sky!" Hannah shouted and leapt for her daughter, latching her arms around the shaking girl.

"I had to. I had to," Skylar mumbled, her arms down at her sides.

Hannah gingerly took the handgun and held it away from her daughter. Skylar finally turned her head and Hannah hopped away.

"Are those night vision?" Hannah said. "For a second I thought something had happened to your face."

Skylar swallowed. "Mom, can we go home now?"

"We have to get Gabe first. He ran so I didn't have to," Hannah said, her head going down, visibly ashamed.

Skylar's chin quivered. "Nothing's catching him. Not even those fucking birds."

"Birds?" Hannah said.

Skylar explained, quickly, leaving out much, including the horrible insects. If she never mentioned them, never thought of them again in her lifespan it would be too soon. Already her mind was working to stash certain elements of the day for later, if she was lucky, later would never come.

"He'll be going to the fire," Skylar said. "So will the other bikers. One other one already got ate. It was incredible. These are his goggles." Skylar pointed to her face as she rambled.

"Shh. Shh, it's okay."

In the resumed quiet of the forest, only the crackling of branches and the occasional gentle splash of water came to them. Whatever they were going to do to get out of there, standing still was not going to help.

"How about we go back near the fire, maybe up in that good tree—"

Skylar interrupted her mother. "That's where the birds came."

"Right. A different tree then. We get close to the fire, and you watch the dark while I hold the gun."

Skylar nodded to her mother. "There's another bullet thing over there, too. Unless they took it."

Moving slowly and carefully, Skylar led the twosome toward the gentle glinting of the firelight. The flames had shrunk much over the last few minutes.

"How will Gabe find us if there's no fire?" Skylar said.

Hannah paused mid-step. "Right. I'll grab some logs if you point them out."

This made Skylar huff. It was all so meaningless. All these little things they were doing, and what if they could never go back? What if that had been a one-way door?

"Mom, how do we get out of here?"

Hannah sighed. "Point out a couple good pieces for burning, okay?"

"But—"

"One thing at a time."

Skylar looked around the forest floor that now seemed busy with all the wrong bits of wood. She directed her mother to numerous sticks. Hannah held up her arms—gun in her waistband—and Skylar began loading.

Skylar gasped. A three-inch bug inched along the wood and onto Hannah's arm.

"It's okay, let's just move," Hannah said, facing forward, looking at nothing of the dark, dark world beneath the forest's green ceiling.

Skylar started forward, understanding that her mother was forcing calm into a situation where normally she'd be far from it. They were now moving much faster than they had. Every few seconds, Skylar brushed away phantom bugs she felt land on her skin. The fire came into view and Hannah started running. Skylar lifted the goggles to watch her mother drop the wood onto the slow-burning front tire of the Harley. Hannah then began brushing frantically at her arms and beneath her torn shirt, her body jitterbugging all over; that calm held only as long as was of absolute necessity.

A splash of water stole Skylar's attention. She lowered the goggles and scanned the surf. Back and forth, back and forth, she saw nothing until she did. There, not fifteen yards away, two wideset amphibian-like eyes bulged upward, above the surf, and were closing in on the beach by the burning bike and the helpless survivors of time travel.

In fact, those eyes were so damned terrifying, she didn't notice the motorcycle engine screaming their way.

TWENTY

Keeping the water visible to his right was the only way he had of knowing if he was going in the correct direction. As he moved clumsily through the darkness, the first and most lasting thought that came to Gabe was of dogs, and how the short things that had chased him were very much like dogs. When he was twelve, he'd been playing near some huge warehouses a couple blocks from the airport. Those warehouses were some of the only one- and two-story buildings left in the city. Though they didn't know for sure, the general guess was that keeping them short allowed for better take-off and landing visuals. In one of the industrial parking lots, Gabe and a group of friends had been playing ball hockey. They'd lost three balls throughout the morning, and finally, right around the noon hour, they'd lost the fourth. If they wanted to continue playing, one of them had to go over. Gabe was volunteered because of his track team status, as on the other side of the fence, rumor had it there were five massive rottweiler dogs monitoring the grounds. The second rumor, and the truth of this not one boy questioned, was that the dogs had been trained to go for the thighs so their victims bled out, but often settled for genitals.

The other boys watched in silence as Gabe scaled the twelve-foot chain-link fence. He moved slowly, quietly, an eye constantly over his shoulder. He saw no dogs. At the bottom, he clung in place, his toes six inches from the pitted asphalt below, as if the dogs were warned by ground vibration rather than sound. Terrified, he touched down. He saw no dogs. The first ball had gone over and bounced against a doorframe, rolling it back toward the fence. Gabe ran to it first. He snatched it up and tossed it, skying it high above the fence, sending three boys off chasing it. Adrenaline had invaded and he didn't have full control of his strength. He scanned around him for the second ball, and then for danger. He saw no dogs. That second ball had bounced along a huge roll-up door about twenty feet from the fence. Gabe snatched and spun, launching it over the fence without losing a stride. The third ball sat in a puddled dip; all its orange fuzz gone brown. Gabe looked around as he continued his next dozen steps. He was feeling better, almost certain now that the dog stuff was all made up to keep boys out. He bounced the ball three times on a dry spot. Moisture stamped ovals onto the dry asphalt. Gabe cocked back and flung the ball, barely clearing the fence. He took to jogging after that, as the final ball had come to a stop about 50 meters from the fence. Thoughts of dogs were now secondary as he began wondering if his mom had a pizza in the freezer. He bent and picked up the ball. It was as if it had been psychically connected to a dog collar. Instantly, feet scrambled around a corner in a tight turn, a monstrous rottweiler breaking toward him, slobber streaming back from its incredible jaws. Gabe shot into a sprint, not quite matching the dog; once the dog had fully straightened out, Gabe wasn't close to matching its pace. The other boys began screaming and shaking the fence. One boy shouted, "Throw him the ball!" It took twenty long strides for Gabe to register the idea. The dog was five feet behind him, and the fence was ten feet away. He back tossed the ball hard against the asphalt. The familiar *thunk* noise sounded in the melody of the chase: growling, the doggy gum slapping, the sneaker footfalls against asphalt, and the shouting boys. Gabe didn't look, and once close enough, launched himself at the fence, certain his ass was about to feel teeth. The boys silenced and watched. By the time Gabe got down, the dog had dropped the ball at the fence and was wagging its tail, ready for another toss.

He now wished for a pocket full of balls, though he had no clue if dinosaurs—for he had no doubt about what he was dealing with—would fetch them or if any were still chasing him. So far, one breed had and the other hadn't, which made sense though they all felt a little dog-like and all too smart. He had to mentally veer toward the notion of them not chasing him. Without his cellphone's light, he'd had to slow down and they should have caught him already if they were still after him. Then again, there were always more animals in a forest than one saw.

This idea had him freaking out somewhat. Being a fit, good-looking teenager, he was rarely scared, if ever in recent memory. This feeling just about made him sick to his stomach. It was possible that he might run right into the waiting mouth of some huge, horrible thing and have no way to stop it. A whine hitched up his throat as he stumbled. He took five more steps and stumbled again, whining louder. After three more steps, he tripped and faceplanted on the sandy forest floor. He felt like crying as he pushed to his elbows, his thoughts conjuring the ultimate doggy-saur with huge teeth, big claws, and all the speed of the animal kingdom.

He saw hope then, washing away the recurring canine thoughts.

Beneath the eye-level branches, the flicker of firelight was visible. It had to be the motorcycle. "Thank you," he whispered to the universe as he pushed upright. Behind him, branches began cracking in quick succession. Finding out what made that noise was not something he cared to discover. He broke into a blind sprint. Branches slapped at him as he cut through, his toes hitched on roots, his knees locked at dips in the ground, and still, he remained up and boogying.

He didn't see her, but he heard his sister's voice.

"Mom! There's something chasing Gabe!"

Gabe then saw his mother near the fire. She came rushing toward him, holding a handgun out in front of her like she knew what she was doing. Knowing she didn't know, Gabe launched himself sideways in a Superman dive.

Three four-foot birds waved stubby wing-arms while snapping lizard jaws. Hannah began firing at them. Gabe watched from his elbows and butt, hoping his mother's aim was true, at least lucky. It didn't matter in the end. Three quick bangs—struck or not—had the trio turning and chasing back into the forest.

"Gabe!" Skylar said, before she dropped to her knees and grabbed her brother in a tight, tight hug.

Gabe hugged her back. Hannah came running and joined them. The heat of the gun pressed into Gabe's spine through his shirt.

"Okay. No time for this," Hannah said, abruptly pulling away and standing. "I think we should go back the way we came and find that door, agreed?"

Gabe helped Skylar to her feet. She looked like a bug in the firelight with those goggles on her face. "Are those night vision?" he said.

"Yes. Yes," Skylar said.

"Okay, so where was it?" Hannah said.

Skylar and Hannah both looked around, but the first thing Gabe recalled seeing past the dunes at the door's gateway was the ovular end of the big pond. "That way," he said, pointing.

"How do you know?" Hannah said.

"The water. It only just started after where we came through," Gabe said.

Skylar turned and looked at the distant world. She fidgeted with the dials to zoom. "Boiled! I think I see a sand hill. Can't tell if it's got an opening." She turned her head and said, "Ah!"

Gabe was about to ask what, but a light played over a hill less than a mile away, bringing with it the grumbling roar of a Harley Davidson engine.

TWENTY-ONE

Sheldon was already walking toward the fire when a motorcycle blew by him. He paused, his heart going about a million beats per minute, his mind instantly reliving the removal of his fingers. The pain and terror of that had his legs rooted in the sand.

He'd come all this way for more of that?

The motorcycle's headlights shined like a beam of truth onto the scene, and he watched three figures running toward the woods. His heart seemed to stop altogether at this. That was his family, and the reason they were running was because he was a selfish asshole.

Yes, he'd come for more, all they'd take from him.

He took the Tylenol bottle from his pocket, twisted the cap, and shook the remaining pills into his mouth. He hurried to the pond. Cupped hands brought up enough water to swallow down the pills. He had to move quickly now, but at least when the biker decided to remove the remaining fingers, he'd be high as hell—

Through the surface of the water crashed a huge animal, like a crocodile on steroids. Sheldon spun and began running along the wooded beach, chasing after the light that was chasing after his family. Behind him, grunting and kicking up sand was the huge beast, all teeth and armor.

TWENTY-TWO

Hannah looked to Gabe, thinking they might have to use his speed as a decoy—surely a motorcycle had to slow down in the woods—but also thinking the woods were the wrong way from the sand dune. The three of them were stuck without a plan as the bike's light and growl drew nearer. Tree branches crackled behind them. Big ones. A snout pushed through the foliage into the shine from the firelight. Black smudges rose up from its nostrils like 1980's eyeshadow. Blisters marred its upper lip with small pink boils. It looked to the fire only a moment before turning toward the Laurie trio.

This was the same beast from before.

"Run!" Hannah shouted as she took off. In that split second, she'd made the decision to take a wide route toward the end goal. They couldn't spend any more time in this situation, not if they hoped to survive. Pre-history was no place for city folk.

The biker caught on quickly, trailing on their route. Seconds later, three shots echoed over the quiet plane. Hannah glanced back. Gabe was behind Skylar, running with one hand on her shoulder, lending her some speed. Beyond, the big carnivore was stomping on their tail. A plan struck and Hannah began to slow.

"Hey! Let him catch up!" Hannah said.

"What?" Gabe said as he and his sister peeled past their mother.

"Take a trip!" Skylar said, panic riddling her voice, cracking her words like a pubescent boy's.

"He doesn't see the tyrannosaur!" Hannah said, stopping and putting her hands up, handgun hanging by the trigger guard, dangling from her right index finger. She didn't look back to see if the kids were stopping.

This would work or it wouldn't.

The biker slowed and began screaming non-words. He was like an animal, but he was too focused on her and that was obvious even at a distance. That narrow vision while he sat on that loud, distracting machine had him caught—should the big beast play along.

"Money!" the man barked, so throaty and gravelly it sounded like a grizzly bear trying to speak English. He kicked the stand and tilted the bike as he pushed to his feet. He pointed his handgun, using both hands and stepping in line behind the weapon like a cop. "Money!"

"Yes, okay!" Hannah said.

"Mom!" Skylar shouted, they had run much further along but were well within shouting distance. "Come on!"

The large carnivore leapt from the darkness, stretching its form to its full length. The biker finally turned. It aimed and popped two rounds into the throat of the huge, bloodthirsty maw. Teeth snapped together and the dinosaur jerked its great neck upward, flinging the man in the air. He pinwheeled, sending out a sprinkler shower of hot, hot blood. The cry coming from him sounded almost like he'd said, "Mommy!" He landed heavily and the beast snapped its teeth into his flesh anew.

"Run!" Hannah said, hissing it out as she took her first running step.

She curled back toward the water and Gabe pushed his sister in that direction. They didn't get far before Skylar started shouting, seeing what the others did not thanks to the night vision goggles.

"There's another monster! There's another man!"

"Keep running!" Hannah said, she began firing the gun into the sky, making noise, trying to scare the thing, trying to scare everything. Once she hit a click, she used the button Skylar had told her about and dropped the clip. She pulled the fresh clip from her pocket and slammed it home. She pulled the slider—again at Skylar's instruction. She fired three more shots into the sky.

"That's dad!" Skylar shouted. "The thing's chasing him."

"Run to the dune!" Hannah said, anger filling her. If that sonofabitch Shelly had her children do something selfless now…just let them try to save him, she'd shoot that asshole in the damned head.

"But—" Gabe began.

"To the dune!" Hannah screeched. Beneath the moonlight, Sheldon was clear. He'd obviously seen them. She foresaw what would come next: in order to save himself, he'd run that damned monster toward the kids before peeling off to the relative safety of another direction.

Twenty feet away from Sheldon, Hannah pointed the handgun at him. She could shoot him, sacrifice him to their escape attempt, and he deserved it. She screamed a banshee wail and, instead, aimed for the huge, armored target. She squeezed off four shots. Puffs of sand burst around the thing. It didn't slow.

So close to the kids, so close to her and the path to the world they called home. Sheldon turned his face, as if just noticing how near he was. "Sorry! I Love you!" he shouted and pivoted, burning to his left and the pond, leading the beast away from them.

Hannah stopped dead, blinking. The carnage was almost immediate. The thing turned its great head and snapped its jaws around Sheldon. The snap rang out like firework song.

"Mom!" Skylar shouted.

"Run!" Gabe said.

Hannah blinked around, her focus shifting to the grunting snorts of the huge carnivore racing toward her.

She kicked her feet in the heavy sand, moving as quickly as she'd ever moved before. The dune came into sight. Gabe was waving and jumping at its mouth.

"Go!" Hannah said, having only one syllable of breath to waste.

Gabe hurried through that smoky green doorway that rose, impossibly, from a wall of sand. Hannah felt the beast's stinking exhalations at her back. She was almost there. She glanced behind her. The mucous deep inside the beast's nose was all too clear in that green glow. That close to a dinosaur's mouth was no place for a human mother to be.

The beast lashed out to bite after turning its head, at the same moment Hannah tripped over a rope, winding it around her ankle as she dropped the gun. The big jaws took in a mouthful of sand. Up and running anew, the painted turtle bounced behind her like cans trailing newlyweds' away from the church.

She reached the doorway and passed through.

2047 – THE CURRENT

Kristy Clarke received an instant message to her Chimpy account, giving her the location and make of the downed and riderless Harley Davidson motorcycle the night before. She had to wait on the sidelines until the main hubbub cleared as she hadn't scratched every back on the police department—about one in twenty were honest, un-scratchable—and only about a third of the media acknowledged the sweet touch of her deep, deep pockets.

The investigation didn't travel far onto the quarantined property, even with the chain snapped from the gate. All had halted in consideration for the poison in the land, and a bit for who owned the motorcycle. Most cops, the ones old enough and the ones with old-time ideals, still considered the Black Teeth their brothers in blue.

Kristy arrived with a small entourage of cleaners she kept on retainer—there was no better way to own a politician than to help them out of a messy jam—who typically dealt with problems in hotel rooms or in houses with only an hour or two to work with. Ignoring the health warnings slapped onto the property, Kristy rode shotgun in the lead SUV. They rolled right up to the remains of the house and then parked. The morning was warm but carried the fresh coolness off the mountains that was impossible to find in the city. Kristy inhaled deeply through her nose. So fresh. So lovely.

"Ma'am?" one of the cleaners said. As always, the cleaners wore head-to-toe plastic suits with breather holes at the backs of the necks.

"We're looking for anything recent. Particularly communication devices," Kristy said.

The only real concern here—aside from possibly needing new guys to carry out some of the future heavy lifting—was that something incriminating would get into the wrong hands. The media knew how she did things, mostly, but they had no hard proof and so far, only outlets with non-existent legal departments pushed stories that cast shadows over her empire.

"So, how in the hell does a pile of junk and a cabin get to the point of poisoning three acres of prime real estate?" Kristy asked her driver and righthand woman, Marissa Mark.

"The man who inherited the place was a literal mad scientist," Marissa said.

"That's true? I figured that was bull," Kristy said.

"All true. He was well-respected until—"

A cleaner from up at the cabin shot out through the ruined doorway and began waving. "Come see this!"

Kristy nodded to Marissa, her mouth in a *why not?* expression. They started up the hill and got to about the halfway point when they stopped. The cleaners who had been in the cabin stumbled out right before a trio of disheveled and bloodied people came sprinting, one was dragging a painted turtle on a rope; it popped and bounced with each kick like a skipping ball. They ran past Kristy and Marissa without a word.

"Holy shit!" one of the cleaners said.

The people in white suits scattered as the great cracks and thumps rang out. Behind Kristy and Marissa, the door open bell bing bing bing-ed on the lead SUV. Marissa turned and shouted, "Hey!" as the family climbed inside. Marissa took two steps away from the cottage. Kristy's hand slashed out and grabbed her bicep.

The smashing of the cottage became grunting and sniffing when a massive face poked out through the ruined doorway.

"That's a fucking dinosaur," Kristy said.

Had the beast been dead and fossilized, an expert could've explained conclusively that this specific breed of dinosaur had been, before then, never discovered, though was quite similar to a tyrannosaurus rex. Smaller, but same playing field. It made eye-contact with Kristy before it charged forward, bringing the already flimsy front wall of the cottage with it. Kristy was rooted, frozen.

"Run!" Marissa said, trying to peel Kristy's vise-like grip from her bicep. "Let go!"

The beast covered the distance between Kristy and the cottage in four seconds. It turned its head, exhaling a breath that smelled like the rendering room of an abattoir in August.

"Let go!" Marissa said again.

The huge open mouth swept up Kristy and Marissa between its jaws. It clamped down as it jerked back. Both abdomens detached from their hips, dropping two lower bodies down to the gravel in a gory wash of blood. Tendrils of muscle, veins, tendons, and organs stretched between the two portions. Marissa's feet landed flat and took three of the steps she had been trying to take while Kristy grabbed her, and then fell with a wet gush. Kristy's hips and legs lay flat. The beast lowered its face and popped its head back to move its meal around, and in the process, lost the rest of Kristy. The chewed upper body pinwheeled through the air and landed on the hood of the SUV.

Skylar and Gabe both screamed. Hannah, painted turtle now on her lap, calmly pressed the ignition button and put the vehicle in reverse. She rolled around the second SUV and through the gates without issue— suddenly like a pro. At the road, she turned around and then put the vehicle in park.

"Where are you going?" Skylar said from the shotgun seat.

Hannah did not answer with words, instead hopped out and pulled Kristy Clarke's remains off the hood before climbing back inside. She gave the windshield a bath and the wipers cleared away the excess. Very little was spoken on their way to the parking lot of the Best Western. They took the back way up to their room, passing but a single cleaning lady with a cart. She didn't give them a second glance.

"Thinking we should look at apartments east of the city instead of north," Hannah said, eyes closed, cheek smooshed against a white, white pillow.

The End

For more Eddie Generous, visit jiffypopandhorror.com. Sign up to his newsletter to be entered in monthly horror giveaways.

Check out other great

Dinosaur Thrillers!

Julian Michael Carver

TRIASSIC

After spending many years in artificial hypersleep, a handful of survivors of the exploration vessel Supernova awaken to find their ship torn to shreds. They are unsure of what happened in space or how they crashed into an uncharted planet. Upon exploration of the new world, they soon realize their destination: The Triassic, the first chapter of the Mesozoic Era. A plan is formulated to escape this terrifying landscape plagued with dinosaurs and prehistoric beasts. The survivors soon discover that there may be an even larger threat looming under the trees than just the dinosaurs, threatening to cut their mission short and trap them all forever in the primitive depths of the Triassic.

Hugo Navikov

THE FOUND WORLD

A powerful global cabal wants adventurer Brett Russell to retrieve a superweapon stolen by the scientist who built it. To entice him to travel underneath one of the most dangerous volcanoes on Earth to find the scientist, this shadowy organization will pay him the only thing he cares about: information that will allow him to avenge his family's murder. But before he can get paid, he and his team must enter an underground hellscape of killer plants, giant insects, terrifying dinosaurs, and an army of other predators never previously seen by man. At the end of this journey awaits a revelation that could alter the fate of mankind ... if they can make it back from this horrifying found world.

Check out other great

Dinosaur Thrillers!

Rick Poldark

PRIMORDIAL ISLAND

During a violent storm Flight 207 crash-lands in the South China Sea. Poseidon Tech tracks the wreckage to an uncharted island and dispatches a curious salvage team—two paleontologists, a biologist specializing in animal behavior, a botanist, and a nefarious big game hunter. Escorted by a heavily-armed security team, they cut through the jungle and quickly find themselves in a terrifying fight for survival, running a deadly gauntlet of prehistoric predators. In their quest for the flight recorder, they uncover the mystery of the island's existence and discover an arcane force that will tip the balance of power on the primordial island. Things are not as they seem as they race against time to survive the island's man-eating dinosaurs and make it back home in one piece.

P.K. Hawkins

SUBTERRANEA

Fall, 1985. The small town of Kettle Hollow barely shows up on any maps, and four young friends are used to taking their BMX's outside of town in an effort to find anything interesting to do. But tonight their tendency to go off by themselves may have saved them, and also forced them into the adventure of a lifetime. While they were away, Kettle Hollow has been locked down by the government, and a portal to another world has opened on Main Street. It's a world deep below the ground, a world where dinosaurs roam free, where giant plants and mutant insects hunt for prey. It's also a world where all their family and friends have been kidnapped for sinister purposes. Now, with time running out before the portal closes, the four friends must brave the unknown to save their loved ones. Time is running out, and in the darkened tunnels of Subterranea, something is hunting them.

Check out other great

Dinosaur Thrillers!

Steve Metcalf

OBJEKT 221

Ruthless multi-national conglomerate Allied Genetics is under siege from a paramilitary force for hire. Allied calls in reinforcements and fortifies their crown-jewel property – an abandoned Soviet military facility in Crimea known during the Cold War as Objekt 221. Fortunately for the future of their research, O221 straddles a stretch of rocky landscape that hides a rift – a portal through time and space. Through this rift, Allied Genetics can travel, at will, to the Cretaceous – 100 million years into Earth's past – and bolster their genetic experiments with dinosaur DNA ... something their competitors want to stop at all costs."Objekt 221" is a story blending numerous science fiction elements such as repurposed military facilities, time travel, rogue corporate armies, dinosaurs and the hint of a super-ancient civilization.

Bestselling collection

PREHISTORIC:
A DINOSAUR ANTHOLOGY

PREHISTORIC is an action packed collection of stories featuring terrifying creatures that once ruled the Earth. Lost worlds where T-Rex and Velociraptors still roam and man is now on the menu. Laboratories at the forefront of cloning technology experiment with dinosaurs they do not understand or are able to contain. The deepest parts of the ocean where Megalodon, the largest and most ferocious predator to have ever existed is stalking new prey. Plus many more thrillers filled with extinct prehistoric monsters written by some of the best creature feature authors this side of the Jurassic period.